The Quest of the

. . . 'They are the Seven Magical Treasures of Antiquity, stolen from the Old Gods before they left this world . . . They are all so well guarded as to be impossible to steal – there is no way we can bring them back to Lugh. He has condemned us to death.'

And you will all die, Lugh silently promised, turning away, you will all die!

Also Available:

The Children of Lir
The Last of the Fianna

MICHAEL SCOTT

The Quest of the Sons

Illustrated by Gary Ward

Mammoth

For Clionadh,
the Hylander

First published in Great Britain 1988
by Methuen Children's Books Ltd.
Paperback edition first published 1989
by Mammoth
Michelin House, 81 Fulham Road, London SW3 6RB
Text copyright © 1988 Michael Scott
Illustrations copyright © 1988 Gary Ward
Printed in Great Britain by
Cox & Wyman Ltd, Reading

ISBN 0 7497 0006 8

A CIP catalogue record for this title is available
from the British Library

Contents

'During the Spring and Summer I walk along the cliffs every morning just before sunrise. The air is clear and sharp then, the horizon feels close enough to touch and I can see for miles.

'I have a special spot in the high stones down on the beach; it is dry and sheltered from the sea breezes, and I can sit there and watch the sun come up, first turning the sea the colour of silver metal, making it seem hard and solid, and then softening it again as it changes to warm gold. But I have no time for the beauty of the sunrise, my eyes are elsewhere. I go to the cliffs at that time every morning to look for something – a speck, a sail on the horizon, a glinting metal boat. I am waiting for my brothers to come home.

'For I am Eithne, the sister of Brian, Iuchar and Urchar ... the Sons of Tuireann.

'Some day they will return, and I will be here to greet them. They have been gone so many years now, but I have learned how to wait patiently; I first learned patience when they went away on their quest for the magical Seven Treasures ...'

Chapter One

The Trial

'Yes, we are guilty, we killed Cian!'

In the smoky silence of the great Hall of Tara, the voice of the tall red-haired man in the centre of the room rang out clearly, echoing slightly off the smooth stones and the polished shields of the guards.

'Guilty... guilty... guilty...' The word buzzed around the circular chamber, and those at the back pushed forward to look at the three men standing in the centre of the room. They were clearly visible because they stood in a dazzling shaft of sunlight that came in through a wide circular opening in the ceiling. This spot was called the Circle of Judgement, and only those accused of the most serious of crimes were brought here to be judged by the King and lords of Banba.

The three men were so alike that they had to be from the same family. One of them was taller, slightly older-looking than the other two, but most people kept looking at his brothers, for they were twins, and so alike that it was impossible to

tell them apart. They were tall, slender and quite young, although it was difficult under the harsh sunlight to tell their age. The brothers were all red-haired, but while the twins had bright green eyes, the older brother, Brian, had eyes of stone grey.

'Why?' The voice came from the shadows before them, a strong, powerful voice, deep and rumbling. The voice of Nuada, King of the Tuatha De Dannan.

Brian turned towards the sound, recognizing the king's voice. With the sunlight in his eyes, he could see nothing else in the huge room except his brothers. 'My lord, it was a matter of honour.

10

We killed him because he brought shame on our family, because he insulted our father and sister . . .'

'But three against one,' the king growled from the shadows. 'You had an unfair advantage. Where is the honour in that?'

The lords of Banba rumbled in agreement.

'He ran from us!' Iuchar, one of the twins said suddenly. 'He took the shape of a beast and ran from us . . .'

Urchar, his twin, placed his hand on his arm, quietening him; it would be better for the three of them if Brian alone told the story.

There was movement in the shadows and then a huge man stepped into the Circle of Judgement. He was tall and broad, his head and beard a deep fiery red, and his eyes were bright grass-green. He was dressed in a simple tunic of cream-coloured cotton, belted around the middle with a broad leather belt, and his arms and legs were bare. High on each arm he wore a twisted spiral of gold and there was a simple gold band around his head. He was Nuada, King of the Tuatha De Danann.

But what made Nuada so distinctive was the metal hand that replaced his own hand of flesh and blood which he had lost in battle with the demon, Streng. The hand had been made by the physician-magician Diancecht from plates of solid silver, and it was etched all over with twisting, curling spirals.

The king stretched out his arm, his metallic right hand sparkling in the sunlight, and touched Brian in the centre of the chest. 'Tell me your tale,' he said quietly.

Brian stepped back and bowed deeply, and his brothers quickly copied him; they knew if the De Dannan lords didn't believe their story, then they would be banished from the land of Banba with a price on their heads. Men would come after them for the reward, hunters and professional soldiers – mercenaries – and the brothers knew they would never again know a moment's peace for the rest of their lives.

Brian stepped out of the circle of light, blinking hard in the sudden dimness, and strode up to the huge roaring fire that blazed beside Nuada's great stone throne. The fire was never allowed to die, for legend said that whilst it burned the Tuatha De Dannan would rule the Isle of Banba, and so the Druids, the holy men, made sure it was constantly fed with wood and turf. The young man stared deep into its shimmering glowing depths for a moment before turning back to Nuada. 'My lord, as I tell you our story, let the truth of my tale be judged by the flames . . .'

Nuada walked back to his throne of rough stone and sat back into it, arranging a pillow of thick fur behind his head. He frowned. 'Do you realize what you are saying?'

Iuchar and Urchar looked nervously at one

another and then at their older brother; to call upon the Test of Fire was terribly dangerous. Using the ancient magic, the fire would judge the truth, and if he told only the truth then nothing would happen, but if he lied – even unknowingly – then the fire would consume him.

'I know what I am doing, lord,' Brian said slowly, his clear grey eyes sharp and piercing as he looked around the assembled lords. 'I have nothing to fear, I will tell the truth.'

'If you have nothing to fear, then so be it,' Nuada said, a smile touching his lips. This indeed was a brave young man, and he knew that very few of his older nobles would dare to undergo the Test of Fire . . . he wasn't so sure he would care to do it himself.

Without another word, Brian stripped off his cloak and unbuckled his belt, handing them both to his brothers, and then he undid the thongs of his sandals. Barefoot, he padded to the edge of the flames and then knelt down on the warm smooth stones. He raised both arms and with his palms towards the fire he began to call upon the ancient gods of the De Dannan folk, many of whom had been De Dannan themselves before they had become gods.

'The Dagda and Danu bear witness to me now . . . let Bobd Dearg and Angus Og judge me, and let the Morrigan claim me if I lie . . .'

Sparkles of green appeared in the fire – and

Brian immediately plunged both hands into the flames!

The fire erupted upwards in streamers of coloured flames, mainly blue and green, with tiny multicoloured sparks twisting and weaving around the man's bare arms which were now deep in the flames. But although the flames were shifting and twisting, coiling and turning around them, they remained unmarked, the flesh unburned.

'My lord king,' Brian said slowly and evenly, his eyes closed, his arms still, 'this is how we came to kill Cian. This is the truth. Let the flames be my judge.'

Nuada nodded. 'Begin then . . .'

'My brothers and I were riding here to join your army because we heard of the coming war with the Fomorians. We were riding across the Plain of Muirthemne when we spotted a rider coming towards us, his white cloak streaming out behind him . . .'

And even Nuada, who knew what was about to happen, gasped in astonishment. A change had come over the fire. Instead of the flames lapping around the chunks of wood and the deep rich sods of turf, a picture had appeared in the fire, the image of a stretch of deep rich grassland, bordered in the distance by forests. The king leaned forward, watching intently as a tiny figure on a black horse rode into the shimmering image, a white cloak streaming out behind him.

'We knew it was Cian,' Brian continued evenly, 'and we spotted him about the same time he recognized us . . .'

The rider stopped, his dark steed prancing on the grass. The man seemed undecided, but then he quickly dismounted, turned and ran towards some trees.

'We would have challenged him to single combat – but he ran from us like a coward . . .'

The leaping flames shivered, and the tiny running figure of the man suddenly grew clearer and larger. Nuada and the nobles, who had gathered in silence around the man kneeling before the fire, watched as the man ran into a clump of low trees and bushes – straight into a dozen wild pigs. The animals scattered in all directions, leaving Cian alone in the centre of the clearing. He turned, and seemed to be looking out of the flames at the silent nobles, and some drew back in fright, although they all knew that they were seeing an image of something that had occurred three days previously.

'And then, lord, the man took on animal form in an attempt to escape us . . .'

Cian threw off his white cloak, tossing it into some bushes along with his tunic and sword belt, followed by his sandals. Then he crouched down on his hands and knees on the ground, which had been churned into muck by the pigs. Resting both elbows in the filth, he dropped his head down

16

until his chin almost touched the ground, and he drew his legs in tightly to his chest and stomach. And then something moved across his body, something white and misty. Some of the watchers thought it was merely a trick of the flames, but Nuada's broad face tightened in anger, recognizing what was happening.

Something like a dusting of fine white powder had appeared on Cian's crouching body. As they watched, it thickened and hardened into a crust, like ice or hard snow, until the outline of the man was lost.

And then the crust cracked.

Thin black lines ran across its surface, and chunks of it fell away – to reveal the body of a pig underneath!

The flames roared higher. 'My lord Nuada, Cian had taken on the body of a pig to escape us,' Brian said slowly and evenly. He was concentrating intently on holding the image clear in the dancing flames, and couldn't risk turning to look at either the king or the assembled lords, but he could guess their reactions. The De Dannan folk could take on the form of most animals, but they were an honourable people, and to assume an animal's form – especially that of a pig – to escape honourable combat was a terrible disgrace.

'What did you do?' Nuada demanded, flexing his metal hand, the joints rasping and scraping together. Those who knew him well knew that it was a sure sign of his growing anger.

In the hearth, a log exploded into sparks and the shimmering image quivered into abstract patterns. While it reformed, Brian looked up from the flames and smiled at the king. 'I changed my two brothers into hounds, so that they would be able to spot the magical animal . . .'

The picture hardened again, and suddenly two snow-white wolfhounds, the tall hunting dogs of the De Dannan lords, raced into the clearing, scattering the returning wild pigs in all directions. The identical hounds quickly separated one large pig from the rest and chased it out into the open. As it raced out of the clearing, it spotted the tall figure of Brian and turned towards him. Its long mouth open, its tusks yellow and gleaming . . .

There was a sudden flash of steel, silver and shining . . . and then dark and red . . .

The fire blazed high to show the image of Brian standing over the pig, his sword in his hand, its tip stained with blood. The pig lay on the ground by his feet, a deep cut in its shoulder. The two dogs ran up to stand over the wounded animal, panting, tails wagging.

Brian raised his sword high and moved it through the air in a strange pattern! The three animals were immediately dusted with silver spots that sparkled, glittered and reflected the sunlight in harsh, bright colours. Brian moved the

18

sword again – and three men stood before him: his brothers, Iuchar and Urchar – and Cian. The man was holding his left shoulder and there was blood seeping from between his fingers . . .

'The man begged for his life,' Brian said, his voice sounding tired and weak.

In the flames, the short, wild-haired man with the cruel eyes and the hard mouth fell to his knees, obviously begging the brothers to spare his life . . .

'And we would have,' Brian continued, 'we would have walked away, had he not tried to deceive us. He gave us his word and when we turned away, he tried to stab me.'

The flames roared higher, the pictures moving with them, showing the brothers walking away and Cian raising his dagger high – and then they abruptly turned to smoke and hissing steam as someone emptied a bucket of water over the fire! The sudden shock sent Brian sprawling, sparks of red and gold dancing up along his arms, making his hair stand on end. Thick grey-white smoke billowed around the great hall, causing the lords of the De Dannan to rush coughing and sneezing for the doors, leaving only Nuada and the sons of Tuireann alone in the hall.

A young man stepped out from behind the fire, through the smoke. He was small and dark, his face mean and spiteful and his eyes were a deep muddy colour. He was Lugh and, although he was

19

no more than fifteen summers old, he was already one of the finest warriors in all Banba. He stood beside the smouldering remnants of the fire, a dripping bucket in his hand and glared at Nuada the king.

'My lord, how can you stand there and allow them to dishonour my father's name?' His voice was a whine, sharp and bitter.

'Lugh, you forget yourself,' the king snapped. 'You have nearly extinguished the sacred flame, and how dare you address me in such a manner?'

'They killed my father,' Lugh sulked.

'Aye, and they admitted it. But he brought that death on himself; he disgraced himself and died dishonourably.'

'He was one against three.'

'He was De Dannan,' Nuada snapped, his metal hand suddenly closing into a first, the metallic squeal sounding very loud in the empty hall.

Lugh dropped the bucket and rubbed his thin, long-fingered hands together quickly. 'Well, I cannot say how he died, but he is dead – and these must pay.' He suddenly pulled a long knife from his belt and pointed it at the three brothers.

Nuada reached out with his right hand and closed it around the bronze blade. His hand tightened – and the blade snapped. He dropped the broken knife on to the floor. 'Never draw a weapon in my presence!' he hissed, his metal hand coming to rest on Lugh's shoulder. And the young man, suddenly realising how close he had come to death, nodded silently.

Nuada turned back to the three brothers. He had known them for many years, he had watched them grow up; Brian would be about nineteen or twenty years old now, while the twins would be sixteen or seventeen perhaps. There was a sister also, he remembered, and she would be around thirteen, a very beautiful, but frail girl. Tuireann, their father, had fought by his side against the demon Fomorians, and while the old man had lived away from court for many years now, Nuada still counted him amongst his closest friends.

'You are guilty,' he said finally, his voice sounding tired and weary.

'We admit that,' Brian said quickly.

'And you know the Law?'

'They must be slain!' Lugh snapped.

'Do you presume to be king also?' Nuada demanded angrily, rounding on the young man.

'No, lord, I was merely thinking . . .'

'Do nothing,' Nuada commanded, 'say nothing until I ask you.' The warning was clear in the king's voice.

Lugh gave the smallest of nods; he had no wish to die. He had never got on very well with his father – in fact, they hadn't really liked one another very much. Lugh always thought that Cian was jealous because he was so good at everything, and he hadn't even seen him for nearly

21

two years before he had learned of his death. However, while Lugh had little time for his father, he had even less or any of the Tuireann clan. He had hated them all since the time their sister had refused his offer of marriage. When he had insisted, the boys had thrown him out of the house. He had sworn revenge then – and Cian's death was the perfect excuse. With the brothers out of the way, there was only an old man standing between him and Eithne's hand in marriage.

'The law says that you must die or pay the death fine,' the king murmured.

Lugh opened his mouth to speak, but Nuada's glare silenced him.

'We are about to do battle with the demons again,' Nuada continued, 'and so I think it would be foolish to put to death any of the De Dannan lords, for we will need all the help we can get. You,' he rounded on Lugh, 'will set the death price for your father. And it must not be in coin or cattle, rather make it something which will prove useful in the coming wars. You have until sunset to think of a suitable price . . .'

'There is no need,' Lugh said quickly. 'I already know the price.'

The twins looked nervously at one another, wondering what was coming.

Lugh stepped into the Circle of Judgement, a spiteful smile twisting his thin lips. 'I want you to bring me three golden apples, a shining pigskin, a beautiful spear, a chariot pulled by two horses, seven piglets, a pup and a cooking spit. Oh, and finally, I want you to shout three times on a certain hill.'

'What . . . why?' Brian asked, astonished, thinking that Lugh's mind must be confused by his father's death.

'The seven treasures will help us in the coming battle, and the three shouts will atone for my father's death,' Lugh smiled.

'Is this a trick?' Iuchar said quickly.

Urchar, his twin who knew something of folklore and legend, suddenly said, 'They are the Seven Magical Treasures of Antiquity, stolen from the Old Gods before they left this world.' He looked at his two brothers, trying hard to blink back the tears that stung at the back of his eyes. 'They are all so well guarded as to be impossible to steal – there is no way we can bring them back to Lugh. He has condemned us to death!'

And you will all die, Lugh silently promised, turning away, you will all die!

Chapter Two

The Seven Treasures

The old man sat on a broad flat stone on the beach listening to his three sons. He was tall and frail, his long face wrinkled and worn, and there was a tremble in his fingers. But though age had lightened the colour of his hair, it was still red and bright.

'And so we must find and return these seven treasures to Lugh before he will consider himself paid for the death of his father and to satisfy De Dannan law,' Brian finished.

Shaking his head slightly, Tuireann looked out across the gently lapping waves. His speckled hands tightened around his carved walking staff until his knuckles turned white, and his chest rose and fell as he took deep breaths to calm his anger.

'I'm sorry . . . we're all sorry . . .' Iuchar began.

Tuireann smiled sadly. 'I'm not angry at you. I cannot say what you did was right or wrong because I was not there. I cannot judge. But I know that Cian was an evil man and brought heartache and sorrow to many people and I know his son

Lugh has inherited his evil ways. Why,' he added bitterly, 'he alone is the cause of this coming war with the Fomorians.'

'How?' Brian asked surprised.

Tuireann smoothed his cream-coloured robe and sighed. Without looking at his sons, he told them what he knew. 'You know we have been paying taxes to the demon-folk for many years now? Well, although no one liked paying, we all realized that there was nothing we could do, at least not while the giant, Balor of the Evil Eye, remained their king. You my sons, are young, you have never seen him, but he is a foul hideous creature, with three eyes on a face that is as ugly as this stone!' Tuireann slapped the large flat pockmarked rock he was sitting on. 'He sees through two of his eyes while the third eye in the centre of his forehead remains closed. But in battle two men with long sticks push the eyelid open, and then whoever or whatever he looks at bursts into a ball of flame, or freezes into a chunk of ice depending on the demon-king's mood.' The old man shook his head. 'We cannot fight that evil power – our magic is not as powerful as the demon-folks, and that was why we paid our taxes. Of course we have been secretly gathering our forces and in a year or two we would have been ready. But then Lugh ruined everything by killing one of the tax collectors – and so we are at war again.'

'Can we win?' Brian asked softly.

Tuireann shook his head. 'I don't know; if we had more time it would be different . . .' He looked at Urchar, who had trained for a time as a bard and knew all the lore and legends of Banba and indeed most of the known world. 'Tell me about these treasures Lugh wants you to bring back.'

Urchar settled himself on the beach and, with the flat of his hand brushed a section of sand smooth. Then with his fingers he began making a series of shapes which his twin Iuchar finally realized was a map.

'The Seven Magical Treasures are scattered all across the known world,' Urchar began, 'and it will take us many years travelling to reach even the first, never mind all seven.'

'We don't have that sort of time.' The old man shook his head. 'Tell me about the treasures,' he repeated.

Urchar's finger moved until it had reached the furthest right hand point on his rough map. 'The first of the Treasures is here in the Orient in the Land of the Dragon King. The Three Golden Apples grow in the Garden of the Hesperides and there they are worshipped as tokens from the gods. Only three grow at any one time and it is said that if all three are plucked at once then the tree will die and the surrounding countryside will be struck with plague and famine.'

'Why are they so special?' Brian asked.

Urchar looked at him and smiled. 'A tiny piece from one of the apples will cure even the most serious wounds. But if the apples were made into a cake or paste then they could be used to cure hundreds of wounds.'

Their father tapped the sand with his carved stick. 'What else does Lugh want?'

His son's finger moved across the map again, stopping close to the centre. 'He wants the Shining Pigskin which is kept by the King of the Greeks. It has the power to cure all diseases.' He looked at Iuchar, knowing what he was about to ask. 'The first treasure cures wounds, the second cures diseases.' His twin nodded silently; the brothers were so close that they often knew what the other was thinking.

'What about the next treasure, the Spear?' Brian asked.

Urchar's finger moved to the right and down. 'The Spear is a terrible weapon, it can destroy armies, melt stone, even turn the seas to steam. It is here,' – his finger stabbed the sand – 'in the Land of the Persians.'

A huge wave rolled in, and droplets of water splattered across the three young men and their father, speckling the map in the sand. The tide was turning, coming quickly up the long shallow beach.

'The next treasure is here,' Urchar continued quickly, moving his finger across to an island at the foot of a long leg-shaped piece of land, 'in the Kingdom of Sicily. It is a Chariot that was crafted by the last of the elven blacksmiths, and the two horses that pull it are half-breeds, having been bred from the magical steeds of the old gods and horses from our own world.' Urchar looked up at his father and smiled. 'Both the horses and the Chariot can ride like the wind on land – and on water!'

'The Seven Piglets,' Brian reminded his brother, watching the incoming tide.

'The Seven Piglets,' Urchar said, moving his finger to the left, stopping where the vast Western Ocean joined the Middle Sea. 'We shall find them here at the Pillars of the Sun. They are truly magical creatures, the last of their kind. They are tiny, fat and pink, like ordinary animals. They can be killed and used to feed an army for its evening meal, but in the morning they will be alive and whole again. And so long as their bones are kept intact they can be killed again and again and again . . .'

Tuireann nodded. 'If we had them the demons would never be able to starve us, there would never be another famine.'

Brian agreed with him. 'It seems as if all of these treasures would help us greatly in the battle with the demon-folk.'

'But if you bring them back,' Tuireann said bitterly, 'it will be Lugh who will get the credit for saving Banba.'

'Father,' Brian smiled, 'if we succeed in bringing back the Treasures, then no one will forget the Sons of Tuireann. Think of the saga it will make.'

'I'm not finished . . .' Urchar reminded them. He stabbed his finger into another part of the crude map. 'The next treasure is a pup kept by Irud, the King of Irud. It is a small delicate-looking animal, but because it is so beautiful, any other animal that looks at it falls down senseless. Flocks of birds fall out of the heavens in wonder at its beauty.'

'But how useful would something like that be in time of war?' his twin asked.

'One day it will be the finest hunting dog in the world. All the birds and beasts will acknowledge it as their leader. It would enable us to control our enemies' beasts, or we could command the birds of the air or the animals of the field, even the fishes of the sea, to attack the Fomorians.' He paused and added, 'We would no longer have to hunt if we had such an animal, since we could call the creatures to us.'

'What about the Cooking Spit?' Iuchar asked.

His twin grinned. 'Always thinking of your stomach, eh?' His finger moved back to Banba and stopped off its northern shore. 'That can be found on Fairhead Island, which is somewhere off the coast between Banba and Alba, although no one has ever found exactly where. But any meat that is put on to the spit will never go cold, nor will it ever diminish. A man could live forever off the tiniest bird that had been cooked on that magical cooking spit.'

'So those are the Seven Treasures,' Tuireann said slowly.

'But there's one other thing,' Brian said quickly.

'I thought there were only seven treasures?' the old man asked.

His son shook his head. 'Seven treasures and one task. We have to shout three times on Midcain Hill.'

'Aaah,' Tuireann breathed, 'Midcain, the Hill of Silence. It is a place deep in the Land of the Fomorians . . .' He jabbed at Urchar's map with the point of his walking stick. 'And this hill is guarded by four of the demon-folk, Midcain and his three sons. Because of an evil deed they did when the world was young, they were placed under a geasa – a spell – to keep the hill silent and sacred to the White God who will come. On pain of death, no one speaks on Midcain Hill.'

Iuchar smiled ruefully. 'And we have to shout on it.'

'They will stop you,' the old man said, his voice soft and cold.

Iuchar laughed. 'Well, they will try . . .'

'They are giants,' Tuireann said. 'Once an ice-serpent from the frozen wastelands came down and attempted to nest on Midcain Hill. But the noise it made upset the old man Midcain, and so he took his staff – which is really nothing more than a tree trunk – and struck the ice-serpent a single blow, killing it instantly.' Tuireann looked at Iuchar, his faded eyes distant and sad. 'Can you stand against that?'

The young man shrugged. 'Well . . . the three of us together . . .' he began.

'There are four giants,' Tuireann said slowly. 'Midcain the father and three sons, Conn, Corc and Aedh.'

The tide boomed again, and white froth washed in over Urchar's map.

Brian came slowly to his feet. 'We must go,' he said sadly. He looked down at his father. 'Can you tell us how we can get to all of these strange lands?' he asked. 'Do you know of any magic that will carry us across the waves?'

'I have heard of such spells,' the old man said slowly, looking out to sea, 'but it is a powerful spell indeed, and I'm afraid I have neither the strength nor the knowledge of such magic.'

'Does anyone?' Brian asked.

'There is only one person I know who has something which might help you . . .' Tuireann began and then stopped suddenly.

'Father . . ?' Brian asked, alarmed at his father's expression.

Tuireann pointed silently.

The three young men turned to look out to sea – and gasped in astonishment. A craft was sailing in directly towards them, a long low, sleek craft that burned in the early morning like fire. A fantastical head – part fish, part dragon – had been carved into

31

the prow and its two eyes glowed a deep dark red. There was a single square sail set directly amidships, and it was deeply bellied as if a strong breeze were pushing behind it. But the breeze was coming from behind Tuireann and his sons – it should have been blowing the craft away from the shore, pushing the sail in the opposite direction!

'Sorcery!' Urchar breathed, closing his hand into a fist, but leaving his forefinger and little finger raised, making the ancient sign of protection from evil magic.

Brian turned back to his father. 'What is it? Who is it?'

'It is what I was going to tell you about,' the old

man said slowly. 'Only one person in Banba has a magical craft capable of travelling across the waves . . .'

Brian turned back to the sea. The magical boat was much closer now, and they were able to pick out details on its flowing surface. The boat was made from metal, smoothly polished metal that had been joined together without a seam or anything that even looked like a bolt. Brian shaded his eyes against the glare and then he suddenly recognized the small dark young man standing behind the dragon-shaped prow. 'Lugh!' he breathed.

Tuireann nodded. 'It is his craft.'

The vessel crashed up on to the beach with a scraping of metal on stone, and then the wind died from its square leather sail. Tiny lines of white and red fire ran along the etchings cut into the sides of the craft and danced on to the damp sands sparkling with soft buzzing sounds.

Lugh vaulted over the side and dropped down lightly on to the sand. He deliberately ignored the old man, although custom and good manners indicated that he should have at least bowed to Tuireann. There was a look of contempt and malice on his thin pale face. 'There has been a change . . . and because of it Nuada tells me I must give you my craft, the Navigator,' he said sharply.

No one said anything, but the three brothers moved in around the young man, while the old man remained sitting on the rock, his eyes distant, looking at the horizon.

Lugh suddenly realized that he was surrounded, and he felt a cold chill run over his body. He attempted a smile, but only his thin lips moved. 'The demon-folk will arrive in twenty days time – so you have until then to discover and return the treasures.'

'There is not enough time,' Iuchar said softly.

'That is why Nuada commanded me to give you my craft,' Lugh snapped. 'It was created by the Old Ones using the last of the High Magic.' He touched the boat's metallic sides with the tips of the fingers of his right hand and shivered as a warm tingle ran through him, tingling down to his feet and then into the ground. 'It travels with the speed of the wind. All you have to do is to tell the figurehead where you want to go . . .' His voice trailed away at the brothers' hard looks, and their father's complete disinterest. He looked around again, and then jumped with surprise as a wave washed in around his sandalled feet, the cold water startling him. 'If you tell me when you wish to start I will have it made ready . . .'

'If we only have twenty days,' Brian said coldly, 'we will take it now.' He turned back to his father and embraced him warmly. 'We will return soon,' he whispered in his ear.

The twins also embraced their father. 'We will make you proud of the name of Tuireann.'

'I already am,' the old man said, swallowing hard.

The three sons of Tuireann turned the metallic craft around until it was facing out to sea, and then began to heave it back into deeper water.

'Hey ... what about me?' Lugh said suddenly. 'I've sailed here from Banba's western shore to bring this to you. How am I going to get home again?'

'Walk!' Brian said, and hopped into the bobbing boat.

Chapter Three

The First Treasure: The Golden Apples

The Navigator skimmed the waves, the water parting before its red-eyed dragon prow. A shell of magical power – faintly blue when the sun shone through it at sunrise and twilight – surrounded the craft and enclosed the brothers, so that although they were travelling at an incredible speed, they felt nothing, not even a breath of wind on their faces.

The Land of the Dragon King was at the end of the world, and without their magical craft the sons of Tuireann might have travelled for the rest of their natural lives and never reached it. With the High Magic of Navigator however, they arrived in the warm waters of the Orient on the morning of the third day after leaving Banba.

Brian commanded the Navigator to stop in the mouth of a deep wide bay in sight of a village of straw and bamboo. Although it was just past sunrise, the village was awake, and the smells of the cooking fires drifted out across the warm water, the scents of the strange spices making the brothers' mouths water and their stomachs rumble.

'I'm hungry,' Iuchar said, running his fingers through his curly red hair.

Urchar, his twin, nodded in agreement. 'I could eat a horse.'

'We'll eat later,' Brian said, still watching the village. 'There are no fishing boats,' he said then.

'So . . ?' Iuchar asked.

Brian glanced back over his shoulder. 'This is a fishing village,' he explained slowly, 'there should be boats . . .'

'They're out fishing!' Urchar said suddenly.

His older brother nodded with a smile. 'And when they return they'll have to pass us.'

The twins suddenly nodded in understanding. If they were spotted now and the alarm was raised, their chances of stealing the Three Golden Apples were reduced almost to nothing. They knew that if they were to stand any chance of success they needed the element of surprise.

Brian looked into the sky, and then measured the marks of the seaweed on the golden-sanded beach. 'The tide will turn soon . . . we have less than an hour . . .'

'We could sail off-shore and lie in wait until evening,' Iuchar suggested.

Brian shook his head, no. Puzzled, Iuchar looked at his twin.

'This is a metal craft,' Urchar explained patiently, 'a boat of polished golden metal. When the sun drops low in the sky we will reflect the light like a mirror, and the longer we wait the more chances there are that we will be discovered. Although this village looks very insignificant, it is a stop on an important trade route, and a merchant fleet could sail around the headland at any time. No, we need to move now,' he said decisively.

'But what can we do then?' Iuchar asked.

'We'll have to shapeshift,' Urchar said, with a sudden shudder. Shapeshifting was something he detested.

Brian nodded in agreement. 'Something fast, but powerful . . .'

'A bird . . ?' Iuchar said.

'Eagles,' Urchar added quickly. He loved birds and had at one time or another taken all their shapes and flown the skies with them. 'Golden eagles; they're both fast and powerful.'

Brian nodded. 'Golden eagles, then.'

The three brothers stood together in the centre of the craft, joined hands, then they bowed their heads and prayed to the Old Gods, the Gods of the Tuatha De Dannan. Urchar began to speak, slowly building up a word-picture of a golden eagle, a tall, bronze bird, with golden eyes and a wing-span as broad as a man was tall. And then, with the image in their minds, they began to shapeshift.

Tiny tendrils of steam rose from their skin, as if they had just stepped from a hot bath, and sparks of blue-green energy darted across their fingertips and made every hair on their head, arms and legs stand on end. The steam thickened but, instead of drifting away, it cloaked the brothers in a blanketing mist. The steam deepened in colour, from a pale white to a deep grey, completely concealing the three young men. For what seemed like a long time nothing happened, but then there was a crack and blue-green fire rippled through the fog, spitting, hissing and sparking. The thick grey-black fog dispersed, burned off by the blue-green fire . . . and the brothers were gone. In their place were three golden eagles.

The three huge birds took to the air with a tremendous clap of their powerful wings, and climbed into the brilliant blue sky, heading inland, in towards the Emperor's palace and the Garden of the Hesperides.

Brian took the lead. He only had the vaguest idea where the capital of this strange land was, so he climbed higher and higher into the sky, until the horizon began to curve, and the air beneath his sleek feathers was chill and thin. And then, with his eagle's sight, he looked down across the land of the Orient. He could only see now in stark shades of black and white, but he could see in incredible detail.

He noticed the mountains first, tall grey-black

mountains that crawled all across the land, their upper slopes and crests snow-covered; in Banba no mountain top remained covered with snow in summer. Then he spotted the long straight lines running across the countryside, the lines white against the softer grey of the land. He puzzled over it for a moment and then adjusted his sight, following one of the lines until it came to a village – a tiny cluster of straw and bamboo huts – and then he abruptly realized that he was looking at a road. The country was lined with roads. In his own land, the only roads were around Tara, and even then they were pitifully crude when compared with these smooth, sanded stretches of white stone.

He circled lower, looking for the broadest road, sure that would lead to the capital. When he had found it, he beat his powerful wings again, climbing higher, but with his eyes still firmly fixed on the ribbon of road. And there in the distance was the glint of polished stone and the glitter of glass. He had found the capital city. Folding his wings, he dropped lower, into the thicker air, and then began to fly towards the city with his brothers close behind him.

The sun had almost reached noon by the time the three sons of Tuireann flew over the towering walls of the city. Immediately their nostrils – beaks – were clogged by the countless thousands of mixed odours, the strongest being those of the people and then the cooking smells. The odours were strange and exciting, and more than anything else told them that they were in a land very foreign to them.

Brian headed in towards the centre of the city, making for what seemed to be a very impressive building – indeed, it was so big that he was tempted to call it a city within a city. They flew across a broad plaza and then over the second set of high walls into this inner city, marvelling at the delicately carved, life-like statues guarding the ornate metal gates. Within this city, in long lines along the paths and roads, there were hundreds more carved statues of warriors and wizards, tigers and dragons, and no two were the same.

The smells drifting up to the brothers were different now – they were sharp and spicy, bitter with strange herbs and sweet with the scents of strange juices. Even the very scent of the ground was different; in Banba the soil was deep and rich and dark, here it smelt thin and hard, sharp with the burnt smell of sand.

Suddenly Urchar, who knew more about magic than his brothers, scented something different. His sleek eagle's head came up sharply and he swung around in a sharp turn to follow a curious odour of burnt, scorched metal – the scent of magic.

Urchar followed the strange bitter smell to a high wall that had been topped by spikes. Beyond this wall was a second, and then a third, and then there was a deep moat of blue-black water, in which strange shapes stirred and gave off a horribly foul smell. Beyond the moat was a fourth wall, also topped by spikes. But these defences had been meant to stop creatures that walked, and they were no hindrance to the birds. The three golden eagles flew to the top of the fourth wall and settled down on to the bars between the spikes.

The Garden of the Hesperides was surprisingly small but it was filled with the most exotic flowers, trees and shrubs from every land in the known world. Some were incredibly rare, huge flowers and orchids that had grown when the world was young, strange ferns with leaves that were neither vegetable nor animal, ugly wrinkle-leaved plants whose flowers looked like the heads of dogs, tiny clumps of star-shaped flowers that grew so closely together that they looked like one huge plant, and whose scent was a deadly poison. There were trees of every known wood, some tall and slender, others short and many-branched, and there were others whose wood looked like stone or metal.

And in the centre of it all was the apple tree.

It was disappointing to look at, small and stunted, its branches twisted, its trunk gnarled. It was set a little apart from the rest, and the ground around it seemed to have been deliberately cleared of all other growth, and there were the rotted remains of dozens of apples on the ground around the trunk. Although it was out of season, there were apples – large red and green apples – on the tree, weighing down the branches. A light breeze moved the leaves and branches, parting them, and then the noonday sunlight blazed brilliantly in three places – the three golden apples.

The golden apples were much bigger than ordinary fruit, each one as large as a child's head. They were perfectly smooth and round, and a deep rich bronze-gold colour.

The three brothers looked at one another. Although they were unable to speak in their bird-form, they knew what they were going to do. They would each fly in, wrap their taloned claws

43

around the branches holding the apples – and rip the whole branch off. Holding on to the branch would be easier than holding on to the apples themselves, they had decided. Then back to the boat with as much speed as possible. The birds spread their wings and Brian was just about to give the signal to move off when the first guard stepped out from behind the tree.

The man was small but broad, and his armour of polished wood and leather made him look even broader. His face was wide and flat, with high prominent cheekbones and uptilted eyes, and to the brother's surprise, his skin was a faintly yellowish colour. Besides the flat curved sword in his belt, he was carrying a small curved bow and there was a full quiver of arrows on his back.

He stopped when he saw the three huge birds perched on the high wall and, turning his head slightly, but keeping his eyes on the birds, he spoke in a strange spitting language. A second guard appeared immediately. He was taller than the first, wearing similar armour, but carrying a lance that was as tall as himself. The two men spoke quickly together, and then the first guard reached down into his quiver for an arrow . . .

Brian launched himself off the wall in a flurry of feathers. His powerful wings pushed him towards the guard so quickly that the man hadn't even time to bring the arrow to the bow before the bird's hard claws wrapped themselves around the bow and ripped it from his grasp. His razor-sharp beak snipped the string on the bow and he dropped it at the guard's feet, completely useless now.

Meanwhile, the twins attacked the second guard. Iuchar flew in towards his face, making him bring up his arm to protect his eyes, and then Urchar snatched at the spear with both claws and his beak, tearing it from the man's hands. He flew over a thorn bush and dropped the spear into the centre.

The first guard now had his sword free and was slashing at the three birds, screaming all the time in his rough, ugly language.

Suddenly a broad-headed arrow parted Urchar's tail-feathers. He screeched in alarm, and his pounding wings lifted him high into the sky over the garden. He hovered and looked down, and spotted a third guard lurking in the bushes, with another arrow in his bow, ready to fire. As he watched, he saw the man stand up and turn towards his twin who was busy defending himself against the sword-wielding guard. Urchar folded his wings and dropped like a stone.

Too late the archer saw the golden-feathered bird dropping down on to him. He attempted to raise his bow in time, but the eagle landed with all its weight on a broad branch directly above his head. The branch snapped down under the weight and rapped the man across the forehead, sending him sprawling to the ground, unconscious.

The sudden movement distracted Iuchar's attacker for a moment – long enough for the bird to dart in, and clap his huge wings together around the man's head. Shocked and dazed, the guard staggered around in a half-circle – and ran straight into a tree, knocking himself unconscious.

Brian found himself facing the largest of the guards, a huge man who fought with two broad swords, which he shifted, twisted and twirled with amazing speed and skill. Curiously though, he didn't seem to be pressing home an attack on the bird, he seemed satisfied to keep the bird away from the apple tree.

He's waiting, Brian decided, he knows we're after the apples and he's waiting for something – or someone! Flapping his huge wings, he lifted up and out of the garden, to hover on the warm scented air, his sharp eyes searching the garden. He caught the glint of metal over by the wall, and suddenly realized that the guard was about to be changed. He wasn't sure how long either he or his brothers could hold the eagle shape – shapechanging was an exhausting magic – but he knew that they would be hard-pressed against three fresh guards. He threw back his head and screeched aloud and Iuchar and Urchar rose up out of the garden to join him. Brian turned to face the approaching guards, his brothers turning with him. When they spotted the threat, they nodded.

As one, they folded their wings and dropped

down on to the remaining guard, their beaks wide, their claws extended to tear. The man was terrified; one eagle was bad enough, but three of them together, and all of them with razor-sharp talons and beaks. Even if he managed to chop down one, the guard knew the others would get him. Screaming, he turned to run, and then one of the birds struck him full in the back, its claws rasping along his armour. The force of the blow lifted him up off his feet and tossed him head first into a bush. As soon as he touched the white-green leaves, long vines lifted themselves out of the ground and wrapped themselves around the man's body, holding him as fast as a fly in a web.

But his scream had attracted the attention of the approaching guard, and they came running down the path, bows ready, shouting for more guards. Somewhere in the distance, a huge gong began booming. The alarm had been given.

The Sons of Tuireann wrapped their claws around the three branches holding the apples and then flapped their huge wings, lifting themselves into the air, tearing the whole branch off the tree complete with its precious fruit. They rose into the air – but slowly, slowly – for the apples were surprisingly heavy. Arrows buzzed around them, one actually bouncing off the branch in Iuchar's claws, nearly making him drop it in fright.

More guards came running, the sounds drifting

47

up to the birds, who were still climbing into the air, their voices like the buzz of distant insects.

Suddenly there was silence.

Brian looked down, and with his eagle's sight spotted the tall yellow-skinned man in the pale yellow robe standing beneath the apple tree. He was merely watching the three birds, not saying anything, his lined and wrinkled face not moving, his eyes small and black. He folded his arms into the sleeves of his robes – and then something like a smile touched his thin lips. Brian felt something cold touch him then, for that smile was the most frightening and evil thing the young man had ever seen. Turning his face to the sea-breeze, he beat his powerful wings and headed after his brothers.

As the last of the three huge golden eagles flew away, the three daughters of the Dragon King ran into the Garden, drawn by the booming of the alarm. They were tiny creatures, and all identical, although they had been born a year apart. In her own language the eldest girl was called Spring Morning, and she was seventeen summers old, and her sisters were Summer Evening and Winter Night. The three girls stood around their father and looked at the ruined apple tree, and then turned to look at the distant specks of the birds.

'Bring me back my treasures,' the Dragon King of the Orient said in a chilling whisper and turned away. The girls nodded and bowed deeply, holding their bow until their father had gone, and all his

48

guards with him, leaving them alone in the Garden of the Hesperides.

Spring Morning turned to her sisters and placed the palms of her tiny hands on their foreheads, and they both placed a hand on their elder sister's forehead. The change that came over them happened so quickly that a small bird that had landed on the broken apple tree fell off its branch in fright when it looked up and found three dragon-creatures crouched on the ground below it.

Except for the colours of their scales, they were identical. They were long low creatures, with broad flat heads, like those of serpents, and with a ridge of needle-sharp spines running all along their backs from the tip of their pointed noses to the ends of their tails. They were covered in triangular plates of hard shell, and their short stubby legs were tipped with four claws as long as a man's hand.

Spring Morning, a pale silver-blue in colour, spread her almost transparent wings and seemed to drift upwards into the air. Moments later, the other two dragons, one a warm gold, the other a silver-black floated up to join her. They flapped their large wings and set off for the coast . . .

The Sons of Tuireann were exhausted. The fight with the guards had been tiring, and the apples were heavier than they had expected and they had to work constantly to hold on to the eagle shape. If their attention wandered even for an instant, then

49

they would change back into their human form
– and crash hundreds of feet to the ground
below. But they also knew they couldn't rest,
they wouldn't be allowed to escape easily –
someone or something would be sent after them.

It was Urchar who spotted the dragons. He
was lagging behind his brothers, his wings
heavy, the branch in his claws like a chain
dragging him to the ground, and he knew that if
he didn't rest soon he was going to
automatically change back to his real shape and
fall . . .

He suddenly felt the tingle of magic. It was a
pins and needles type of feeling he usually got in
his fingers and toes when someone was working
some magic or calling up a spell close by. But he
was high in the sky, there was no one close
enough to affect him so . . .

Unless . . .

Urchar turned his slender eagle's head and
spotted the three coloured dragons coming in
high and fast. He screamed a warning to his
brothers and then dived for the ground.

The three dragons split up, one to each eagle.
They knew they had the advantage since the
eagles couldn't use their claws, and were almost
defenceless. Also, as well as their talons and
teeth, the dragons had one other weapon . . .

Winter Night, the silver-black dragon followed
Urchar down, and as he fell, she suddenly spat a

fist-sized ball of flame at him! It missed, but it had been close enough to singe his wing feathers.

The golden dragon, Summer Evening, followed Iuchar. Unlike his brother, he went up . . . up . . . up, hoping the dragon would not be as strong as he was, and would be unable to fly in the thinner air. She spat fire at him, three tiny specks that grew as they approached him. He lunged to one side, darting into a thick white cloud, and heard one of the balls sizzle off the edge of the damp whiteness.

Brian followed his brother's example and went down as the pale silver-blue dragon, Spring Morning, spat fire after him. There was a forest below and he darted into it, relying now on his speed and quick thinking to escape. Inside the forest, the smaller and lighter dragons would be much more agile, but he had speed and strength, and also his eyesight would be far keener than the pale slit-eyed dragons. He peered through the trees and saw Urchar being chased by the silver-black dragon. He saw his brother twist to avoid a ball of fire and then come darting into the darkness of the trees. Brian lifted the branch in his claws and allowed the slanting sunlight to reflect off it, using it like a torch to attract his younger brother's attention. Meanwhile, beyond the edge of the forest, Spring Morning and Winter Night were hovering together, obviously planning something.

In the skies above them, Summer Evening was

gradually burning away the cloud Iuchar was hiding in. She was spitting fire at it, and when the balls struck the cloud, they hissed and sizzled and immediately died, but not before they had burnt off a little of the cloud. However, inside the tiny damp grey shell, Iuchar had realized that the dragon's fireballs were becoming smaller and weaker, and he guessed that she was running out of flame. With his keen eyesight he peered through the thinning fog and watched the dragon's long throat working, her mouth opening – and nothing happened. She was out of fire. And the eagle burst out of the cloud heading straight for the dragon!

Surprised, the dragon hesitated for a moment – and then Iuchar was upon her. She opened her mouth to bite, but the eagle was already rising, using the golden apple on the end of the branch like a club. As he rose past, the solid apple struck the dragon in the side of the head, dazing her. Iuchar twisted in mid-air and suddenly settled on the dragon's back and closed his wings. The dragon – with the eagle on its back – dropped like a stone. The creature's mouth opened to scream – and then Iuchar suddenly found himself holding a struggling young woman. He was so shocked he dropped her, and she fell crashing into the trees, her silken gown catching in the branches, leaving her dangling high off the ground, kicking and struggling, but otherwise unharmed.

Enraged by the treatment of their sister, Spring Morning and Winter Night flew into the wood, searching for the other two eagles. When they caught them they would burn them to a crisp, and then take care of the third eagle.

The silver-black dragon suddenly spotted one of the golden eagles perched on a branch not more than a hundred paces ahead. With a scream of joy she darted off towards it, feeling the rumble of fire deep in her throat. She twisted and turned through the weaving branches, and then spotted an opening through the trees. Gathering her strength, she made a dash for the gap . . .

She was almost through the opening when she spotted the second eagle. It was to her right, and it had a branch firmly clamped in its claws and beak, and the branch was bent almost in half. She saw the eagle release the branch . . . saw it come snapping around back into its original position directly across her path . . .

The branch caught the dragon just below her front claws, winding her, and the shock was enough to make her resume her human shape. With a scream of terror, Winter Night fell to the ground, sinking up to her knees in the soft earth.

Spring Morning, the eldest of the three sisters, was more cautious. She perched on a branch, her spiked tail wrapped around the tree trunk, watching the largest of the three golden eagles. Almost as if it had felt her presence, the bird

54

turned its golden head to look at her. The Dragon Princess shivered suddenly, and wondered what human shape lurked beneath the birds covering. She began to work her long sinuous throat, gathering fire in her cheeks. She knew if she could catch the creature by surprise, she would be able to make him resume his human form, and then he would be no match for a dragon. The dragon opened her mouth slightly, breathing in air, making the fire hotter . . . and then something large and golden distracted her. She looked up – just in time to see a large golden apple dropping down on to her head!

With a squeak of surprise, Spring Morning swallowed the fire, and the sudden shock and belly-ache knocked her backwards off the tree, leaving her dangling upside down by her tail. And then she slowly began to regain her human form, her claws softening, the nails shortening, her arms drawing back into her body. Her teeth sank back into her head, the jaw pulling in, the cheekbones melting, and her mass of jet-black hair reappeared. The young girl desperately fought to retain her dragon shape. She knew that once she lost her tail she would fall to the ground and snap her neck.

There was a whisper of feathers, and then iron-hard claws ripped into the soft fabric of her gown, lifting her upwards, pulling her away from the tree, and setting her gently on to the ground. The Dragon Princess stared into the deep bronze eyes of the eagle, and then the bird was gone.

She saw it soar up into the trees, and pick up a bright golden apple in its claws, where it must have left it while it had saved her. It rose into the pale blue sky and was joined by two more birds, each one clutching a golden apple. Spring Morning looked around, seeing her sisters, one dangling from a tree, another stuck in the boggy ground, but they were safe; the birds hadn't killed them.

And then, although she knew the creatures were stealing her kingdom's most treasured possessions, she raised her tiny slender arm and waved the birds farewell.

The great golden eagles circled around her once and then headed off towards the coast. The Sons of Tuireann had the First Treasure.

But unknown to them, across the seas in Banba, Lugh was sitting in his darkened rooms, a magical mirror before him, watching their every move. He cursed as they settled on to the metal craft and resumed their human shapes – and he swore that next time they would not succeed so easily!

Chapter Four

The Second Treasure: The Shining Pigskin

Two days later, the Navigator sailed into the warm salty waters around the Island of the Greeks.

The sky was cloudless and the brothers sweltered under a huge milk-yellow sun. They lay stretched across the three oar-benches, soaking up the warm sunshine. They had remained in the shapes of eagles for too long and were still stiff and sore after it, and every movement made their aching muscles crack and complain.

Brian was the first to realize that the Navigator had stopped moving. He sat up and peered over the edge of the craft and spotted the red-gold line of cliffs and the sparkle of white stone buildings in the distance.

'We've arrived,' he announced.

The twins sat up and, shading their eyes against the glare of the sun, looked at the Greek Islands. They looked peaceful and very beautiful, floating in water that looked too blue to be real. However, both Iuchar and Urchar, used to the lush greenery of Banba, thought the islands themselves were a little too pale and dusty for their liking.

'What's the Second Treasure?' Brian asked, running his hands through his bright red hair, settling a slender metal band around it to keep it away from his eyes.

'The Second Treasure,' Urchar said, 'is the Shining Pigskin of the Old Gods, which is now kept in the treasury of Tuas, King of the Greeks. The golden-skinned pig was slain by one of the Old Greek Heroes, but when he realized that it was rich in the ancient earth magic, he skinned the beast and used it to make the most powerful magic.'

'It can cure diseases, can't it?' Iuchar asked, remembering what Urchar had told them.

Urchar nodded. 'Even if a man is suffering from a fatal disease, he only has to be wrapped in the skin and his illness will be healed.'

'With that in his possession, a man could be like a god,' Brian said in wonder.

'It could be used for great good,' Urchar said seriously.

'Or for great ill,' his twin added.

Brian nodded. 'Well, first we have to find it, and then we can worry about how it can be used. Now . . . we have to get into the King's treasury . . . and I don't suppose *that* will be too easy,' he added.

Urchar suddenly laughed. 'That will be no

problem,' he said. 'About this time every year, a great Festival of Learning is held in the Court of King Tuas. The finest poets and singers, storytellers and bards from all the known world gather here to stand before the king to recite or sing or tell him a tale from the history of their own land. The king's scribes record these songs and tales and add them to the king's huge library . . .'

Brian nodded quickly. 'We could pose as storytellers, and that would at least get us into the palace, and I suppose we could break into the treasury later that night . . .' He stopped, seeing the delighted smile on his younger brother's freckled face.

'There's no need for anything like that,' Urchar hurried on. 'When the king has heard all the tales and legends, stories, poems and sagas, he will choose a winner from the piece that most pleased him. The prize for the winner is to fill a cup with jewels or precious metal from the king's treasury.'

'Maybe we could ask for the Shining Pigskin,' Iuchar said.

'He won't give that.'

'Well, we'll just have to take it,' Brian said grimly.

'You have to be chosen as the best storyteller,' Urchar reminded him.

Brian smiled. 'I don't think we have to worry about that. After all, we are the Sons of Tuireann.'

He stood up in the boat and looked up at the red-eyed dragon prow. 'Navigator, take us in to shore.'

Because they were the last to arrive, they were the last to speak and so it took the Sons of Tuireann seven days before they finally stood before Tuas, the King of the Greeks.

Brian, followed by his brothers, walked up to the king and bowed deeply. 'My lord, I am Brian, eldest son of Tuireann, and these are my brothers, Iuchar and Urchar. We hail from the Land of Banba in the wild Western Ocean.'

Tuas, a small thin man with deeply tanned skin and a large hooked nose, smiled pleasantly. 'You are welcome to my court.' He looked past Brian to his brothers. 'Twins, I see.' In his country, twins were considered lucky. His vague brown eyes looked at Brian and he smiled again. 'I have heard of your land. Perhaps you will tell us a tale from its past?'

'If that is what my lord wishes.'

Tuas waved his hands together. 'No, no, it is not what I want, the choice is yours.'

Brian smiled. He couldn't help liking the gentle, shy-looking man. 'Well, my lord, we will tell the tale of the First Invasion of our land.'

Tuas nodded. 'I would like to hear it.'

So Brian, with help from his brothers, told the tale of the Princess Caesir Banba who had come from the Land of the Egyptians to the tiny island

60

that would one day grow into the Land of Erin. The audience listened in an almost breathless silence, and even the other bards and storytellers were caught up in the tale. And when Brian and the twins finally finished their tale, there was no doubt as to who had won the prize. Everyone in the hall began to applaud and even the guards pounded the wooden butts of their spears against the ground.

Tuas stood up and came down to the three brothers, his arms outstretched. 'I have never heard a story told with such feeling,' he said. 'I felt as if I were there. Has your land many such stories?'

'The history of our land is one long tale,' Urchar said with a proud smile.

'You know what your prize is – but afterwards, when all of these have gone, I would like you to stay and tell me more tales from the Land of Erin.'

'My lord, I am afraid we cannot stay,' Brian said regretfully. 'We are on a quest, and time presses on . . .'

Tuas nodded. 'I understand.'

'But we would like to return when it is completed,' Urchar said quickly.

'You would be very welcome.' The king raised his arm slightly and a huge warrior in a metal breastplate and wearing a helmet that hid most of his face strode over. 'This is Aneas, the Captain of my Guard, he will conduct you to the treasury.'

The king then reached out and took a large metal goblet from a table by his side and handed it to Brian. 'You may fill this with whatever treasure you desire – except of course my magical treasures.'

'But we would like to see them,' Iuchar said softly, 'perhaps we could use them in a story.'

Tuas laughed. 'Yes, perhaps you could. And I think I would like to hear that story some day.' He nodded to the huge guard. 'Follow Aneas, he will show you the way.'

Without speaking, or even looking at them, the Captain of the Guard led them down into the depths of the palace, deep into the tunnels that ran beneath its marbled floors. There were dungeons and cells, deep pits and strange echoing chambers, and there was an armed and armoured guard every ten paces.

They passed through a long room that held nothing but the scroll-like books and tablets of the Greeks, thousands lined in a row; the collected histories, the folk and fairy tales of every land in the world, and with every step the brothers' admiration for King Tuas increased. Here indeed was a man of learning – and in Erin a man of learning was honoured and held in as much regard as a warrior.

Finally, Aneas stopped before a huge wooden door that was studded with bolts as big as a man's hand. Two men stood outside, big men with pale blue eyes and long blond hair worn in twisted plaits. They were wearing breastplates of leather sewn with metal squares and armed with long double-headed battle-axes. The brothers recognized them as northern mercenaries. They were cruel and vicious warriors who hired themselves out to whoever would pay most and so long as they were paid, they remained loyal and devoted.

Aneas nodded to them and they silently pulled back the heavy metal bolts and pushed the door open. Light . . . soft, warm and golden, sparkling, glittering, twinkling light washed out over the men.

The Sons of Tuireann had never seen a treasury before, and so they hadn't really known what to expect, and the sight before them took their breath away.

'I thought it would be messy,' Iuchar said in an awed whisper. 'You know, everything tossed around, dumped in corners, just thrown in . . .

The treasury of the King of the Greeks was laid out neatly and in perfect order. The room was a long high one, almost perfectly square, and without windows. Gold was stacked in one corner, with silver and bronze beside it, bars, ingots and coins neatly separated. Then there were the jewels, bags and boxes of them, all neatly marked and labelled with their names, colours, purity and country of origin. Beside them were the

cups and crowns, rings, necklaces, armbands,
knives and swords, all made from precious metals
and encrusted with jewels. There were carvings in
green stone from the lands to the east, tiny figures
made from ivory from the Dark Continent to the
south, and brightly-coloured carpets and rugs from
the lands to the east and south.

The brothers walked slowly down the centre of
the room, their mouths and eyes wide and round.

However, when they reached the back wall,
they found it was surprisingly bare with only a
few items hanging on it: yet each one was strange
and different. There was a sword, two small
knives, a crown, a cup, a wooden stick, a string of
glass beads and, tossed over the back of a chair, the
Shining Pigskin!

'They're all magical,' Urchar whispered,
'magical treasures from the past, each one with a
special power.'

'Well, we're only interested in one,' Brian
murmured. He looked over his shoulder and found
that the huge guard was moving slowly towards
them. 'Look, you two keep Aneas busy, and I'll try
to get the Pigskin.'

While the twins kept the guard talking, asking
him what was the most valuable treasure, or what
they should take in their goblet, Brian turned back
to the magical treasures. He wondered what they
all did. Urchar would know, he knew everything
about folklore. He glanced back over his shoulder,

but Aneas was busy lifting a stack of gold slabs so the two young men could slide out some of the rare white gold at the bottom of the pile.

Brian reached out and touched the Pigskin. It was warm as flesh and smooth as silk beneath his fingers. He felt his fingertips begin to tingle with the power in the skin. He glanced up again to check on Aneas, but the guard was still busy. Brian grabbed the Pigskin and bundled it under his arm. He was wearing a long woollen cloak and he hoped that if he kept his left arm close to his side, the Pigskin would be invisible.

But as soon as he lifted the Pigskin from the back of the chair a thin high screeching started. Brian looked down at the chair in amazement. He had been so worried about the skin that he hadn't even looked at the chair. It was tall and high-backed, carved from a strange dark wood and beautifully decorated with thousands of tiny faces of humans, demons, monsters and animals. And now each mouth was open and screaming aloud. He could have kicked himself for being so stupid – the only reason the chair was beside the wall was because it too was a magical treasure. But it was too late to worry about that now.

Aneas reared up, his broad-bladed sword coming into his hand almost magically. He opened his mouth to shout, and then Iuchar cracked him across the back of the head with a bar of white gold. The gold bar bent in a half circle – but Aneas

sank slowly to the ground, a look of surprise on his dark scowling face.

And then the door burst open and the two northern mercenary guards burst into the room, their battle-axes swinging before them. The brothers had seen these warriors fight before, and knew how deadly those axes were. A single blow could cut a man clean in half.

One dashed towards Iuchar and Urchar, while the second moved down the room towards Brian. Iuchar, who was leaning casually against the pile of different coloured gold bars, suddenly pushed against them with all his might. There was a grating rumble and then the wall of metal crashed over on to the guard trapping him beneath its weight.

The second warrior reached Brian before he even had a chance to pull his sword free. The northerner swung his axe around and brought it up and over his head and then down, aiming for Brian's head. The young man flung up his arm – the same arm he had wrapped the Pigskin around. The axe struck the shining skin – and shattered! The shock sent the warrior stumbling backwards, and then Brian was on top of him, his hands reaching for the warrior's throat. The warrior's head hit the floor with a crack, and he went limp.

'Go . . . go, quickly!' Brian shouted, racing for the door. Iuchar and Urchar didn't need to be told, they were close behind. At the door Brian stopped so suddenly that the twins piled into his back sending him staggering out into the long hallway. Facing him was Tuas and a dozen archers.

'I didn't think you were thieves,' Tuas said sadly.

'I told you we were on a quest,' Brian said. 'Well, this was what we were sent for.' He raised the Pigskin.

'You could have asked me,' Tuas reminded him.

'I didn't think you would say yes.'

The king shook his head. 'Never be afraid to ask. Now, however, you have broken the law, and I am afraid that there is only one law for thieves like you.' He turned away, his voice shaking. 'Death.'

As one man the archers drew back their bows and fired.

Brian gripped the Pigskin in both hands and opened it up in front of himself and his brothers. The first wave of arrows struck the Pigskin and shattered. The brothers sheltered behind the skin while the arrows broke or bounced harmlessly off it, some rattling against the wall. Brian risked a quick glance over the edge of the Pigskin just as the archers fired again. He saw the twelve arrows fly – almost slowly – through the air, saw them strike the Pigskin, some breaking, others exploding like the axe head earlier. He saw one strike the Pigskin at an angle, saw it bounce off the low ceiling, saw it cartwheel through the air –

and strike Tuas in the back! The king crumpled to the ground without a sound.

While the guards were distracted, Brian grabbed a torch from the wall and threw it at a second reed-torch high on the wall. He knocked it from its metal holder and both torches fell to the ground in a shower of sparks and burnt out, plunging that stretch of the corridor into darkness. Iuchar picked up two arrows from the floor and threw them like tiny spears, using them to knock down two more torches. With the wounding of the king and the sudden darkness, everything was in chaos and the Sons of Tuireann used the confusion to make a sudden run for escape, knocking down the torches as they ran, leaving only darkness behind them. Once they were out of the corridor where no one knew what had happened, nor what they had done, they were able to make their way slowly and calmly back to the Navigator with their stolen treasure.

They were shivering with excitement and exhaustion as they crawled into the metal boat; they knew how close they had come to death that night.

'What about the king?' Iuchar asked, as the Navigator made its way out of the harbour.

Brian shook his head. 'I don't know. I don't think his wound was serious . . .'

But far away, across the seas in Banba, Lugh,

enraged because the Sons of Tuireann now had two treasures, placed two drops of poison on to the surface of his magic mirror and commanded it to call up the image of the wounded king.

Two days later, Tuas the king was dead.

Chapter Five

The Third Treasure: The Spear

It took the Navigator less than one day to reach the Land of the Persians, and it was night when the red-eyed dragon-prow ship sailed up on to a rocky beach. Overhead the stars sparkled in a purple sky.

The three brothers climbed up the rocky beach to stand on the highest sand dune and stare across the vast plain that stretched before them, the countless grains of sand sparkling silver in the starlight, hissing, sizzling, buzzing together as a light breeze drifted across them. After the greenery of their homeland, it seemed a cruel and frightening place.

Brian turned to his brother. 'And what are we looking for now?'

'A spear,' Urchar said, turning his head away from the breeze, 'a spear with the power to pierce the strongest armour, to destroy even stone. The people of this land call it the Destroyer.'

'It's probably well guarded,' his twin said gloomily, 'perhaps even too well guarded for us.' The three brothers knew they had managed to steal

71

the First Treasure by chance, and it was only by the greatest good luck that they had escaped with the second. Perhaps they might not be so lucky with the third.

'It never leaves the king's side,' Urchar said with a slight smile.

'And who is this king?' Brian asked.

'He is called Pezar. I know very little about him except that he is supposed to be a cruel and dangerous man, who uses the spear for his own evil purposes. He trusts no one,' Urchar added, 'even his guards have guards to watch them.'

'It will be difficult to steal from him then,' Iuchar said.

'But first we have to get into the palace ...' Brian began.

'That will be very difficult,' his younger brother said, 'because the king sees no one.'

'What about prisoners?' Brian asked suddenly, a strange smile on his lips.

Urchar nodded. 'Oh yes, he sees prisoners, Pezar likes to deal with them personally.'

Brian gathered his two brothers together and hurried them back down the beach to their magical craft. When they were all back on board, he said aloud, 'Navigator, take us to the nearest Persian craft.' He saw the strange looks on his brothers' faces and laughed aloud. 'We're about to become prisoners!'

The short stout Persian sea-captain handed the three prisoners over to the black-clad Captain of the Royal Guard.

'We found them floating in the sea, miles from anywhere,' he said nervously.

The huge warrior scowled, glancing at the three pale-skinned, red-haired men, his mouth twisting in disgust. 'There was no craft?'

'None that we could see.'

'And they had no possessions?'

'Only what they wore.'

The warrior in black leather and bronze turned away and looked at the three prisoners again. Something about them puzzled him. They were too confident, too proud to be prisoners, and yes, they seemed completely unafraid, even though they were standing on the docks of a strange land surrounded by heavily armed warriors. There was a tug on his sleeve and he whirled around. 'What do you want?' he snapped rudely.

The fat sea-captain was wringing his hands together. 'Will there be a reward . . ?' he asked, his voice barely above a whisper.

'How long have they been on board your rotten ship?'

'I picked them up this morning,' the man said quickly, the words tumbling over one another.

'Have you fed them?'

'No . . . no, sir, I was afraid . . .'

'Too mean, more like,' the huge warrior

73

growled, glaring at the round-faced man, watching large beads of sweat appear under his turban and roll down his face. 'Well, if you haven't fed them, they've cost you nothing.'

'But . . .'

The warrior allowed his hand to fall on to the hilt of his half-moon shaped sword. 'But what .. ?' he asked coldly.

'Nothing . . . nothing sir.'

'Good. Now begone.' He watched the merchant scuttle away, hurrying back on to his craft, his fat face set in an angry scowl, muttering to himself.

The guard turned back to the prisoners. Well, he didn't know what to make of them, he would have to bring them to the king.

It was a short walk to the palace. Surrounded by guards, the three young men were led up away from the docks, climbing countless steps and meandering through streets that were little wider than alleyways, and each one was festooned with cloths and bolts of rare silks or fine cotton. Merchants sat in their doorways, selling everything from crude metal cups to delicate works of art, and everywhere there was noise, the shouting, screaming, cawing and bellowing of the merchants and their animals, and adding to the din there was the music, the drums, the cymbals and of course the musical language of the Persian folk. But everything stopped as the Sons of Tuireann walked past and the silence they left behind them was almost frightening.

The palace was set a little apart from the rest of the town, down an avenue lined with trees that had to be watered every day, for few green things grew in the hot land of the Persians. There were guards lining the avenue, one standing beneath each tree, as still and as silent as statues, each one holding a long spear with a head like a half-moon.

The palace was a huge white-stone gold-roofed building hidden behind towering walls of darker cream-coloured stone, topped with spikes. The front gates of the palace were huge constructions of solid dark metal, and yet they were so cleverly hinged that they swung open at the guard's slightest touch.

The warrior in black and bronze led the three brothers into the palace gardens, leaving the rest of the guards at the gate, and it was like stepping into another world. There was almost complete silence within the garden, the air was damp, filled with the scents of growing things, and the musical trickle of water. The warrior led them down groves lined with scented trees and bushes, each bush giving off a different odour, some sharp, some bitter, others sweet or sour. They passed trees laden with strange and exotic fruits, the like of which the brothers had never even imagined existed. There was even one fruit that was a bright orange colour! This grove brought them deep into the heart of the garden, finally leading to a large clear open space, in the centre of which was a

75

simple fountain of white stone. The guard cut the ropes which had bound their hands and stood back.

Brian wondered why they had been freed. He rubbed his sore wrists and raised his eyebrows, looking at Urchar, who knew nearly everything about the lore and customs of all lands.

'Only free men may face Pezar, the king. No slaves may stand in his presence,' he explained.

'Silence,' the warrior snapped.

Moments later Iuchar's nose twitched. The sweet, clear scents of the garden had been tainted by something strange, some foul odour. And then Urchar's head came up suddenly – he too had caught the strange smell. They looked at their older brother, and found he was staring off to one side, down a path that seemed to lead in the general direction of the palace. As they watched there was movement along the path and then a figure appeared through the bushes, a small stout figure, clad in bright vivid colours that clashed with the soft shades of green and brown in the garden, dulling even the colours of the flowers and fruits. As the man approached, the warrior in black and bronze bowed deeply, and they knew then that this was Pezar, the King of the Persians.

Pezar was a small man, with a round face and small black eyes. He was completely bald, and had no eyebrows, and this gave him a slightly babyish appearance. He was wearing robes of crimson and gold, and so much jewellery that the brothers wondered how he could carry all the weight. And he was carrying the Spear, but for such a magical treasure it was surprisingly disappointing in appearance. It was as tall as Brian, who was the tallest of the three, but it was nothing more than a simple wooden pole topped with a flat triangular slab of polished and sharpened metal.

The king stopped by the fountain and looked at the three young men, his lip wrinkling in disgust. If it hadn't been for his cruel eyes, he would have looked comical. 'These are the men?' he asked, looking at the warrior.

The guard nodded.

The king turned back to the brothers. 'I know who you are,' he said suddenly, his voice low and hissing like a snake.

'My lord . . .' Brian began, but then the king swung the spear around until the tip was pointing at Brian's throat. And the brothers suddenly realized where the foul odour was coming from – it was drifting off the spear like steam, a mixture of something rotten and smouldering, like burnt metal.

'Do not lie to me,' Pezar suddenly roared. 'Do not even attempt to lie to me. I was warned in a dream about the three men from the west who would come to steal the magical treasures of the world. I've been waiting for you. In my dream, I spoke with a pale-skinned creature who told me

77

that you had stolen the Golden Apples, and he came to me in my dream again this morning and told me that you had killed Tuas of the Greeks and stolen his magical Pigskin.'

'My lord . . .' Brian said, but Pezar didn't even hear him.

'And now you've come to kill me and steal my treasure . . .' The small man was trembling with rage, and the spear in his hand was shaking. 'But you won't steal this!' he snarled. 'Do you know what this is?' he asked turning away, swinging the spear around in a circle over his head until it moaned and little flickers of flame danced on the flat blade. 'This is the Spear of Mithra!' he said triumphantly, and then looked at the brothers as if that was supposed to mean something to them.

'Mithra is his god,' Urchar whispered, without moving his lips, 'the Sungod.'

The king suddenly lowered the spear until its tip was touching the sandy path. A thin thread of steam rose from the tip. As they watched, the spearhead began to glow, first red-hot and then white-hot. The sand began to bubble and melt, and still the spearhead became hotter and hotter, until waves of heat rolled off and forced the brothers to step back away from it. Pezar suddenly lifted the spear and the brothers saw that there was a scorch mark on the ground. The sand was gone, but in its place something glittered. Pezar touched it with the butt of the spear, moving it, and the brothers gasped in shock — the heat from the spear had fused the sand together into a solid lump of dirty glass.

'The Spear of Mithra,' Pezar said again. 'And now that you have seen it you must die!' He suddenly lunged at Brian with the glowing spear. The young man threw himself to one side and the spear passed close enough for him to smell the stench of scorched air. Pezar swung again, but Brian had moved, and the spear crisped a line of white-headed flowers, turning them black and ugly. And then Brian was on top of him. His left hand grabbed the spear just above where Pezar's chubby fingers held it, and his right hand grabbed his throat. With a sudden wrench and push, he pulled the spear from the king's hands and shoved him backwards into the fountain.

It had all happened so fast that neither the twins nor the warrior had moved.

Brian swung the spear around, the metal head hissing on the air and pointed it at the warrior in black and bronze. 'Well . . ?' he asked with a smile.

The man bowed once and backed away, and then he turned and ran back along the path.

'That was easy,' Iuchar said, 'the easiest yet.'

'We still have to get back to the Navigator,' Urchar reminded him, 'and that means we have to make our way through the town.'

'But we have the spear and no one will touch us

while we have that,' Brian said. 'However, I think we should create a little diversion. Now, I wonder, will this work?' he said softly, almost to himself.

He began to swing the spear around his head, moving his wrists to keep it spinning. The stench of burning metal grew stronger and blue-green flames danced across the spearhead, and then with a crackling explosion the spearhead exploded into flame. As Brian spun the spear, it left long streamers of flame hanging on the air.

Brian used the spear like a whip, snapping streamers of fire into the garden, starting dozens of tiny fires. He cracked some towards the palace building. Some fell short and began to burn on the walls, but one landed on the roof and began to melt through the tiles of golden metal.

'Let's go . . .'

There was a splash of water and Pezar emerged from the fountain, soaked through and miserable, his jewelled turban tilted to one side. 'How dare you!' he screamed. 'You touched me! Me! The king of this land . . . I'm wet and . . .' He was so enraged that he began to splutter.

Brian touched the spearpoint into the fountain – and every drop of water exploded into steam! Pezar leaped into the air and ran screaming towards his palace. 'Well, he's dry now,' Brian grinned, and they turned and hurried down the path towards the gates.

'I wonder will the gates be open?' Iuchar said, looking at his twin. Urchar shrugged.

But they weren't.

'What do we do now?' he asked.

Brian walked up to the gates and pressed his hand to them. They were securely locked and barred from the outside. He looked at the twins. 'We could try to find another way out,' he suggested.

Urchar shook his head. 'We've no time. The longer we wait the more time there will be for the army to assemble. And if they call up archers, they can shoot us down from a distance.'

Iuchar nodded. 'I agree.' He looked at his older brother and grinned widely. 'Open the gate.'

Brian stepped back and took a firm grip on the wooden shaft of the spear, and then gently, oh, so gently, he touched it to one of the gate's metal hinges. There was a hiss of steam and a wisp of smoke and the metal began to melt. A bubble formed and rolled to the ground, followed by another and another as the glowing spearhead ate into the hinge. There was a terrible scorched smell on the air, and the twins moved back because the metal was spitting and hissing. As they watched, the metal hinge bubbled away. Brian moved the spear up and pressed it against the middle hinge. Because the spearhead was now so hot it burned through even quicker, long smoking coils of hot metal running down the door. With that gone, the whole weight of the door rested on one hinge, high up, out of Brian's reach. But the weight of the

82

metal door was too much for the single hinge, and with a screaming, scraping, screeching sound of metal the whole door fell outwards, scattering the guards who were waiting outside.

The three Sons of Tuireann hopped over the door and raced down the tree-lined avenue, the guards scattering before them. Brian touched the glowing spearhead to all the trees on the right hand side of the road as he ran past. They erupted into flame, their sap boiling and spitting and hissing, giving off a thick grey-white smoke that drifted across the ground and caused even more confusion.

They ran through the town, the people stopping to look at the wild-haired young men shouting with laughter, but no one tried to stop them. As they hurried down to the harbour, two soldiers raced up, drawing their swords and blocking the street. But when Brian showed them the spear, they turned and ran, throwing themselves into the sea.

'Navigator!' Brian shouted aloud.

Moments later, the gleaming metal craft sailed into the harbour. It didn't even stop while the three young men jumped on board, and then it headed out to sea again. The Sons of Tuireann had escaped with the Third Treasure, the Spear.

Lugh struck his magical mirror with his fist, shattering it. He had done everything to stop the brothers; he had appeared to Pezar in his dream, warning him that they were coming.

And they had still succeeded. Next time would be different, he promised. Next time they would fail.

Chapter Six

The Fourth Treasure: The Horses and Chariot

A day later the three Sons of Tuireann were in the warm waters off the rocky island of Sicily. They were all crouched over a bowl which Brian had filled with clear sea-water and Urchar had worked a little sea-magic over. So now, instead of their reflections in the water, they were seeing the magical image of the treasure they had come to steal – the fairy horses and the metal chariot.

'The horses are the last of their kind,' Urchar said, looking at his brothers. He pointed to the picture reflected on the shimmering water. 'There is fairy blood in them, and although they look thin and weak, they are incredibly strong and can run like the wind.'

Reflected in the bowl, the image of the tall, thin horses galloped down a beach and then veered out over the waves, their silver hooves barely touching the surface of the water.

'And they can run on water,' Urchar added with a smile.

'So how do we steal them?' Iuchar asked.

Urchar looked at Brian. 'Have you any ideas?'

Their older brother stared into the water for a long time and then looked across at the tall cliffs that rose up out of the sea surrounding the island of Sicily. Without turning his head, he said, 'Tell me about the king of this place.'

'Dobar is the king now,' Urchar said slowly, trying to remember the history of this little island kingdom. 'He is a cruel and evil man, who is constantly waging war on his neighbours.'

'Will he know we are coming?'

Urchar shrugged his shoulders. 'I don't know. But remember Pezar said that he had been warned in a dream that we were coming.'

Iuchar nodded. 'A pale-skinned creature,' he said, remembering the king's words. 'But who?'

'Lugh?' Brian murmured. 'But surely he wouldn't . . ?'

Urchar nodded. 'He would. And if he is warning about our coming then there will be a trap waiting for us. We must be ready for that,' he nodded decisively.

'It also means we cannot trick this king,' Brian said.

Urchar touched the bowl of water with his fingertip, and the picture vanished into shivering circles, only to be replaced a moment later by another picture. This time, the chariot pulled by the two horses was galloping down a long sandy beach. When it reached a huge standing stone, it turned around again and raced back up the beach, only to turn again . . .

'The horses are being exercised,' his twin said quickly.

Brian turned around and looked down into the bowl of water again. He nodded. 'Yes, they're being exercised. And look,' he pointed to the long sharp shadows, 'it's either early morning or late evening. So now we know when they are taken out of their stables.' He looked up at Urchar. 'Where are the horses kept?'

'No one knows. They are kept in a secret place, fed and trained there, and only brought out when Dobar needs them.'

'But it has to be some place on the island,' Iuchar said.

Brian nodded and then he pointed to the picture with his finger. 'Look at that tall stone there. If we can find that we know the horses will be nearby. He raised his head and looked towards the prow. 'Navigator, sail us around the island.' The dragon's eyes blazed red and the metal craft rocked on the waves, and then it set off, making for the northern end of the island.

The Sons of Tuireann sailed twice around the island of Sicily without spotting the stone, and it was close to evening as the boat completed its third journey. Brian had commanded it to sail very slowly and now they crept along, with the brothers hanging over the side watching the shore. But twilight had fallen and the shoreline was becoming dusty and indistinct. They were no longer able to make out details. Finally Brian said, 'It's no use, let's wait until morning, and we can try again when we're fresh.' He sat down in the boat, his back against the sail. 'It's a pity we can't just ask the Navigator to take us to the rock . . .'

The metal boat rocked suddenly on the calm sea. Then it changed direction and headed in towards the shore, and moments later the twins both pointed together. They had found the rock!

Brian stood, leaning against the dragon-prow, running his hand down the carved metal scales. 'I'm so stupid, I should have known,' he murmured. He patted the metallic dragon's head. 'Thank you,' he said softly. He looked at his brothers. 'We'll rest now and go ashore in the morning. Sleep well.'

The three young men curled up in the bottom of the craft and almost immediately fell into a deep and dreamless sleep. Although they were close to a dangerous shoreline, they didn't bother to post a guard; they knew the magical craft would carry them away should they be threatened by any danger – either from the shore or the sea.

Brian awoke first, just as the purple sky was lightening in the east and, as usual, he immediately checked their treasures. The three Golden Apples had been wrapped in the Shining

Pigskin and had been stored in a box beside the sail. The Spear of Mithra, because of its size, had been more difficult to store and carry, but Urchar had come up with the idea of tying it to the side of the craft, so that its metal head was always beneath the water, helping to keep it cool.

Iuchar sat up and yawned hugely, followed, a moment later, by his brother. 'I had a dream,' Iuchar said.

His brother nodded in agreement. They always managed to have the same dream. 'I dreamt we captured the chariot and horses, but had no way to take them back to Erin with us.'

Iuchar nodded. 'So I had to ride the chariot back to Banba while you two sailed behind in the Navigator.'

Brian grinned, 'Don't worry, I've already thought of that.'

'What will we do?' Iuchar demanded.

'A little magic,' he smiled. 'Watch.' He leaned over and dipped his hand into the chill water. The twins looked at one another, wondering what he was doing. Suddenly Brian pulled out his hand – and he was holding a fish, a shiny-scaled, bright red fish with black streaks that lived in the Middle Sea. Brian blew gently on the fish and it immediately stiffened and stopped wriggling, then he touched it, once, twice and again, and the fish suddenly changed colour, becoming hard and shiny, almost like a polished stone. Brian dropped the fish on to the metal deck of the Navigator – and it clanged!

Iuchar leaned down, picked up the small fish, and gasped in astonishment. It had turned to stone!

'Give me some water,' Brian commanded.

Iuchar leaned over, filled a small bowl with water and handed it over to his brother. Brian took the fish and dropped it into the water – and it immediately began to wriggle and swim again. Brian smiled, his grey eyes sparkling. 'When we steal the chariot and horses, I'll turn them into stone.'

'And how are we going to fit a stone chariot and two stone horses into this small boat?' Iuchar demanded.

Brian picked up the wriggling fish again, blew on it and touched it, turning it to stone again. Then he slowly drew his little finger down the back of the fish – and it started to shrink! Before their eyes it dwindled until it was no bigger than a fingernail. Brian held up the tiny miniature fish. 'That is how we shall bring them home with us; we'll turn them to stone and shrink them.' He raised his head and looked at the dragon-prow. 'Let's go . . .'

The Navigator brought them smoothly and silently into shore. The twins climbed up the rocky beach and stood watching, while Brian commanded the boat to drift offshore again and remain out of sight until it was called.

'Are you sure this is the beach?' Iuchar asked, as Brian climbed up the beach to stand beside him. He was standing with his hands on his hips, looking around and frowning; it certainly didn't look like the beach they had seen in the enchanted water.

Brian nodded. 'I'm sure.'

'Well then, where are these magical horses and chariot?' he asked.

'There are tracks here.' Urchar was kneeling on the stones and pointing to a patch of sand. There was a single curved hoof print pressed deeply into the sand and, running alongside it, a long thin groove. He saw his brother frown and knew he was going to ask the obvious question – what was the long thin line?

'The chariot wheel,' Urchar laughed. 'You know, you can be so stupid sometimes . . ?'

Iuchar grinned good-naturedly. He knew both Urchar and Brian were much cleverer than he, but he also knew that although he was quite slim, he was incredibly strong, and the finest metal-worker in all Erin. 'Every man has his gifts,' their father Tuireann often said, 'all you have to do is look for them. Never envy a man his own particular gift, but rather pity him because he has not yours.'

Brian pointed up at the cliffs. 'We'll climb up there. We might see something.'

Urchar suddenly looked doubtful. 'You mean climb?'

'Either that or we fly,' Brian said, 'and I don't think we should shapeshift. If we use magic it will alert any magician nearby.'

Urchar nodded doubtfully. He didn't like heights.

'Let's go then,' Brian said and, fixing his fingers into the crevices between the rocks, he pulled himself up.

Although the dark cliffs looked steep, they were quite easy to climb. They were pitted with dozens of handholds and the only real danger was from the hundreds of nesting seabirds which they disturbed as they climbed. The birds would suddenly burst from their tiny caves, startling the brothers, and very nearly sending them – especially Urchar – crashing back to the rocky beach below. The birds would circle around, screaming and cawing at the intruders, and by the time the three brothers reached half-way up the cliff, they were covered with foul-smelling white streaks.

Iuchar laughed at his twin brother's expression as something white plopped on to his head. 'Cheer up,' he said, 'it's supposed to be lucky.'

'Not for me it's not.'

'Sssh,' Brian hissed. The twins looked up. He was standing on a thin ledge peering over the edge of the cliff.

'What is it?' Urchar asked, forgetting his annoyance.

'Look,' their brother invited.

The twins joined him on the ledge and peered over the edge . . . down into a huge war camp!

92

There were hundreds of brightly-coloured tents scattered all across the plain below, and everywhere there were soldiers. To one side, archers were practising, elsewhere men were running to and fro swinging broad-bladed swords at standing poles, while in another place there was a long line of horses, and behind them chariots of all makes and shapes.

Brian pointed to a group of tall men with white hair and pale skin chatting together with another group of small dark-skinned warriors. 'Mercenary warriors from all the nations in the world. Dobar is preparing for war.'

'Against whom, I wonder?' Iuchar said.

Brian shrugged. 'I don't know. All we have to worry about is capturing the horses and chariot. But first we have to find them.'

'I've found it,' Iuchar said with a broad grin. He pointed to a disturbance on the plain below. As they watched, they saw that a chariot, a shining, glinting golden chariot pulled by two smoke-grey, unnaturally tall horses was making its way through the camp. The camp below fell silent as everyone turned to watch.

'That's it,' Urchar said excitedly.

'There seem to be two people in it . . .' Brian said slowly, squinting into the light.

Iuchar, whose eyesight was the keenest, shaded his eyes and concentrated on the chariot. 'There are two men, one is small, and fragile-looking, with skin the colour of silver and hair like glass . . .'

'That will be Dobar's mysterious charioteer. The king is supposed to have captured him from the Little Folk,' Urchar said.

'The other is a huge barrel of a man, with wild hair and a great raggy beard . . .'

'That is the king, Dobar!'

'I'll wager they are going to exercise the horses,' Brian said excitedly. 'Quick, we have to get back down to the beach . . .'

But getting down proved far harder than getting up, and by the time the Sons of Tuireann reached the bottom of the cliffs they were hot and tired and the sharp stones had cut their hands and arms, and scraped their bare legs. Brian and Iuchar reached the bottom first – just as the chariot came pounding up the beach!

The king spotted the two filthy figures on the beach, pointed to them with his whip and the charioteer changed direction, galloping up to them. He pulled the chariot around in an abrupt tight circle that showered the two brothers with sand and pebbles.

Dobar glared at the two young men. 'Who are you?' he demanded rudely. 'What do you want?'

For a moment neither answered, so entranced were they by the chariot and the fairy beasts. The horses were beautiful animals. They were tall and thin, with high triangular ears and eyes that were

slit-pupilled like a cat's. Indeed, with their every movement, they looked as if they had more than a little cat blood in them. The chariot was a masterpiece of fairy-work. Although it seemed to be made of metal, it looked very light, and the framework had been etched and decorated with long lines of hunting scenes. The wheels were very large indeed, and rimmed with metal, and two broad-bladed knives had been fixed into the hubs.

'Who are you?' Dobar demanded again, running a short-fingered hand through his wild beard. His other hand reached for a spear.

'We are the Sons of Tuireann,' Brian said quickly.

Dobar turned pale. 'Then you have come for my chariot and horses,' he gasped, lifting the spear and pointing it at Brian. Then he frowned. 'But I thought there were three of you . . .'

'There are!' Urchar shouted and dropped down from his perch in the cliffs into the chariot, falling on top of the king and his charioteer. The three men went sprawling. Urchar dived on to the king, but the man was incredibly strong and simply picked the young man up and threw him off. The charioteer used the opportunity to lift a strange curling horn to his lips and blow. The metallic cry echoed down the beach, rattling the stones.

Dobar threw back his head and laughed. 'My army will be here soon. You are mine!'

'Not yet.' Iuchar and Brian threw themselves at the king while Urchar snatched the horn away from the charioteer. The strange silver-skinned man's pale grey eyes opened wide in fear and then he turned and ran down the beach, heading back to the camp. He was half-way down the beach when the first of the soldiers appeared, running towards him. He stopped, wondering what to do and, as the soldiers neared, changed direction and began to run back towards the king and the Sons of Tuireann.

Dobar was putting up a fight. He had struck Brian in the chest with the flat of his large, hard hands, and the young man felt as if he had run into a wall. Then Iuchar managed to get a grip on the

96

king's other arm. He twisted – a trick his father had taught him – and the king went down, smacking his head on the stones on the beach. Dazed, he groaned and lay back on the beach with his eyes closed.

A thrown spear clattered off the stones at Brian's feet and another plucked at the cloth of Urchar's cloak. 'Let's go,' Brian called, then he threw back his head and shouted, 'Navigator!'

But nothing happened!

'Navigator, Navigator . . . we need you now!' Brian shouted.

'I can taste magic in the air,' Urchar said suddenly. 'Something or someone is preventing the boat from coming in to us.'

'Lugh!' Brian spat. 'It can only be him, only he would be able to control the boat.'

A flight of arrows buzzed over their heads, some shattering on the rocks and stones, others splashing into the sea around their feet.

'This is it then,' Urchar said, picking up a sword and turning to face the approaching army.

'We didn't do so badly,' his twin said. 'We managed to get four of the treasures . . .'

Brian suddenly burst out laughing!

The twins looked at him in astonishment. He grabbed both their arms and pushed them towards the chariot. 'Who needs the Navigator when we have a horse and chariot that can run on water?' he shouted.

And, as Dobar's warriors ran up to their king, they were in time to see the magical chariot and its two smoke-grey horses gallop swiftly across the waves, heading for a glowing metallic boat that had no crew. What sounded like laughter drifted back across the waves.

The Sons of Tuireann had their Fourth Treasure.

And Lugh had failed again.

Chapter Seven

Two Treasures

'Where to now?' Brian asked his brother as they sailed away from the Island of Sicily. He was leaning back against the dragon-prow.

'To the Broken Kingdom of the Pillars,' Urchar replied.

Iuchar, who was crouched in the bottom of the craft examining the miniature stone chariot and horses, looked up. 'Why is it called the Broken Kingdom?' he asked.

'Because it is split down the middle by the channel that separates the Middle Sea from the Western Ocean, and so part of King Aesal's kingdom is in the northern continent, and part in the southern. And on the cliffs on either side there is a tall golden pillar. In the evenings when the sun sinks low in the west, these pillars blaze with golden light and are visible from afar, and so can guide lost travellers. They are called the Pillars of the Sun.'

The Navigator sailed on through the Middle Sea, making for the Pillars of the Sun and the next treasure. The twins dozed for the short journey, while Brian stood in the prow, leaning against the dragon figurehead, his eyes on the sea and sky around them.

He had decided to keep watch in case Lugh attacked them directly, perhaps calling up a sea-monster or bringing down one of the fabled giant birds of the sky to attack the small boat. Brian knew that Lugh must be getting desperate now, and that if he was going to stop them he would have to do it soon.

It was evening as they approached the channel through which all ships had to pass to reach the Western Ocean. The cliffs on both sides of the channel were alive with sparkling lights, and it was only as they came closer that they realized the cliffs were lined with hundreds of people holding aloft torches and burning reeds.

'I don't like it,' Iuchar said, standing up. He moved forward to the prow of the ship, his hand shading his eyes, looking up at the crowds of people. 'They're so quiet,' he added, his own voice falling to a whisper.

'They are expecting us, they have been warned,' Urchar said slowly, and for some reason he felt more frightened now than he had at any other time during their adventures.

Brian agreed. 'Lugh again.' He looked at the lines of silent people, their eyes all sparkling in the flickering lights as they looked down. He wondered what was going to happen. Would they be attacked when they came into shore, or would they be allowed to land and then imprisoned?

'Perhaps they're not waiting for us?' Iuchar suggested as the Navigator slipped silently in towards the shore.

His twin made a rude noise. They were now so close they could see individual faces in the deepening gloom, and it was very apparent that everyone was looking at them.

'Perhaps they don't know it's us?' Iuchar added hopefully.

'They know,' Brian said shortly. 'There can't be that many metal boats with a set of twins and another man floating about the Middle Sea.'

'They could attack,' Urchar said.

Brian shook his head. 'If they were going to attack, I think they would have done so by now. They could have placed archers or spearmen on the cliffs above to rain arrows or spears down on top of us before we even got close.'

'So we're going in?' Iuchar asked.

Brian nodded. 'We're going in.'

The Navigator moved in to the pier and bumped against the wooden sides, and in the silence that followed, the lapping of the water sounded very loud indeed. There was a sound from above and then all the people who had been lining the pier moved back. Suddenly an old man looked down on to them, his hair and beard startlingly white against the deep tan of his skin.

'Welcome, Brian, Iuchar and Urchar, the Sons of Tuireann,' he said with a shy smile.

Even though they had been expecting it, they were shocked that the man even knew their names.

'Oh, don't look so startled,' the old man said. 'We've been expecting you. I have been having these nightmares for the past few days warning me about the arrival of these three terrible wild men from the west. Every night a small pale creature with ugly eyes came to me in my dreams, urging me to attack you, but strangely, the more he warned me against you, the more I wanted to meet you, to judge you for myself. So I used a little of my own magic – and discovered the truth. I know why you had to set out on this difficult and dangerous quest. Oh, and I am Aesal, King of the Golden Pillars,' he added, with a quick, nervous smile.

Brian, Iuchar and Urchar climbed up the smooth wooden steps that led up from the water's edge to stand before the king. The old man was very tall and thin, and because he was so thin, it made him seem even taller than he was. His face too was long, which gave him a slightly sad expression, but his eyes were bright and sparkling. Brian opened his mouth to speak, but the king raised his slender hand. 'Everywhere you have gone, you have taken your treasure, and left behind you angry and bitter people,' he said quietly. The king

102

turned away suddenly, and the people holding the torches moved back – and there, on the green-tinged damp stones were seven wicker baskets. The king picked up one and opened it slightly. The Sons of Tuireann crowded around to peer inside . . . and found they were looking at a fat little piglet.

'The Seven Piglets,' Urchar whispered, glancing at the six remaining baskets. It could be nothing else.

Aesal nodded. 'The Seven Piglets. They are magical creatures descended from the huge wild boars that once roamed this world, and they still have a little of that ancient magic in them. They may be killed and eaten, like any other pig, but if their bones are kept together and placed in this basket, then in the morning when the basket is opened, the piglet will be found to be whole and alive again.' He handed the basket to Brian. 'And they are yours!'

'You're just giving them to us?' Brian asked, amazed.

Aesal smiled. 'Not just me; my people all helped me make the decision.'

Brian was shocked. 'Thank you . . . thank you all . . . But why?'

'If we didn't, I'm sure you would find a way to take them, and someone would be sure to get hurt, or even killed. And no treasure – no matter how magical – is worth that price.' The king turned to

103

Iuchar and Urchar. 'Will you load the baskets into your craft?' he asked, and then he turned back to Brian. 'What is your next treasure?'

Brian frowned, counting off the treasures they already had and those they still had to find. 'There is a pup in the Land of Irud that will one day grow into a monstrous hound and will be the finest hunting dog in the world. It will be so proud that all the birds and beasts will acknowledge it as their leader and so strong as to be able to defeat armies.'

Aesal nodded. 'I know the animal.'

Brian bent his head slightly, but said nothing, wondering what was to come.

'The King of Irud – and his name is Irud – knows you are coming,' Aesal said very slowly. 'Your enemy, whoever he is, has warned him, as he has warned all the kings of your coming. Now Irud's army lines the beach where you must come ashore and they have orders to kill you on sight. They have even brought their engines of war that can hurl stones and boiling water and oil down on to the beach, hoping to sink your craft before it even gets close to the shore.'

'We must still try to take the pup,' Brian said.

'I know that, you are on a quest.' The king nodded in understanding. 'Irud is with his army, camped on the beach in the midst of his men. He didn't want to leave the animal at home, lest you crept past him and stole it from there, so he brought it with him. It is kept in Irud's own tent. However, the tent is surrounded on all sides by his personal guards, huge men from the Dark Continent to the south. You will never get past them.'

'We will try.'

'But Irud has sworn he will defend the pup to the death.'

'We will still try to take it.'

'You will have to kill Irud to do it,' Aesal said sorrowfully, and then he added in a whisper, 'He is married to my daughter; they have been married for a month.' He looked at Brian, his eyes glistening with moisture. 'And I don't want her to become a widow so soon.'

Brian looked over the edge of the pier at his brothers settling the seven small baskets in the Navigator. He turned back to Aesal. 'We won't harm Irud – I promise you.'

'Thank you,' the king said.

Brian climbed down the ladder and stepped into the metal boat. Night had closed in and when he looked up at the king, he found his face was now no more than a blur surrounded by the white of his hair. 'We shall be back by the morning.'

He turned to the prow of the ship. 'Take us to the Land of Irud, please.'

It was nearly midnight before the metal craft stopped and bobbed in the inky waters of the Land of Irud. Like the Pillars of the Sun, light burned on the shores, but these were not warm welcoming

105

torchlights, but rather sparking watchfires on the beach, huge piles of driftwood deliberately set alight to warn off trespassers, tiny glowing sparks spiralling to the heavens. And everywhere the dancing flames sparkled off metal – helmets, spears, swords, shields. The beach was covered with soldiers.

The three brothers leaned over the side of the Navigator looking at all the lights on shore. Luckily, there was no moon and the night had clouded over, so they were invisible against the blackness of the sea.

'How do we get past the guards,' Iuchar whispered. Although they were still a good distance away from the beach, they all knew how easily sound carried at night, and especially across water.

'Could we try shapechanging?' Urchar asked.

Brian shook his head slightly, and then, realizing his brothers couldn't see him, said, 'No. The king's magicians would know immediately if any magic was attempted this close to shore.'

'There must be thousands of soldiers,' Iuchar mused, watching all the shapes moving before the fires. 'Irud must have hired mercenaries from nearly every land.'

Brian was just about to reply, when he had an idea. And although he said nothing, both his brothers sensed his sudden excitement.

'You have a plan?'

'An idea?'

Brian nodded, and the twins could see his teeth gleam whitely in the darkness as he smiled. 'The king has hired mercenaries from every land,' he said slowly, 'and surely that means that the men will not – could not possibly – know one another . . .'

'I don't see . . .' Iuchar began.

But Urchar nodded quickly. 'Of course. So all we have to do is march right through the camp.'

'Exactly. We will pass ourselves off as mercenaries.'

'And what do we do when we reach Irud's tent, which is guarded by his special warriors from the Dark Continent?' Iuchar asked. 'We cannot disguise ourselves as one of them – they will all know one another.'

'We'll take care of that problem when we come to it,' Brian said. 'Navigator, take us in to shore over there.' He pointed down the beach away from the moving soldiers.

The metal ship shifted and then moved silently in towards the beach, heading for a particularly dark spot. It stopped when its metal bottom touched stone. One by one the Sons of Tuireann slipped over the side, careful not to splash and then, moving their feet and legs carefully through the water – not lifting them out – they moved up on to the beach. When they were out of the water, they rubbed their leggings as dry as possible with leaves and, with Brian in the lead, they boldly made their way into Irud's camp.

As Iuchar had said, there were hired soldiers from every nation in the world there. Small and tall, thin and broad, some wild and savage, dressed in furs, others well-dressed, looking like princes. There were weapons of every sort, from short swords no bigger than knives, to swords that were even taller than the men who carried them. There were spears and knives, axes, maces, morningstars, clubs, bows and arrows. And everywhere there were shields. Some were of straw, others of wood and hide; some were plain and simple, others were wild and extravagantly shaped, brightly-coloured with crests and symbols painted on to them.

The three young men walked through the army, their heads bent, appearing deep in conversation. They had brought their own swords and shields and didn't look at all out of place. No one even bothered to look at or question them.

The king's tent was in the centre of the camp, a huge brightly-coloured pavilion of heavy leather over a wooden frame. There was a bright light burning within, visible through the chinks in the leather, and the shadow of a man appeared across the leather, moving to and fro. But seated and standing around the tent were ten of the largest men the three brothers had ever seen. They were from the southern Dark Continent; tall, proud men with skin a deep lustrous brown, hair tightly curled

and eyes of coal. They spoke in a strange singing language that had clicks and stops in it. Each one was taller than Brian, the tallest of the three brothers, and they were all broader, their muscles rippling under their smooth skin. They carried huge oval-shaped shields, covered in the skin of a strange spotted beast, and spears that were nearly as tall as themselves with broad leaf-shaped blades.

Urchar touched Brian on the arm and whispered in his ear 'Now what?'

Brian looked at the men, wondering what to do. They were alert and although they were talking quietly together, and two were drinking from a flask, their eyes were constantly moving, and they seemed alert to every sound drifting up from the beach.

Back on the beach, two drunken soldiers began fighting and the clash of swords brought the ten men around to the front of the tent, their spears ready, their shields on their arms. Only when they were satisfied that it was nothing unusual did they drift back to what they had been doing.

Brian had seen enough – and he had had an idea. Turning his back on the tent, he looked towards the sea and whispered a single word, 'Navigator!'

And far out to sea the metal craft turned in the black waters and headed in towards the shore. Moments later it had been spotted and all the guards lining the seashore began shouting at once.

'They're coming . . !'

'They're coming . . . a boat . . !'
'There's a boat coming . . !'
'Boat coming!'
The whole camp was in an uproar. Huge bonfires, which had been covered in fish-oil, were lit up, making the beach as bright as day, and enormous war drums began pounding. The ten huge warriors didn't even wait – they headed off towards the beach at a run.

'They'll be back in moments,' Brian whispered, coming to his feet and racing towards the king's tent.

Irud, King of Irud, threw back his tent flap and stepped out into the warm night air. 'What's going on . . ?' he demanded, and then gulped as an ice-cold sword rested against his nose. A young red-haired, grey-eyed warrior glared at him. 'You're coming with us,' he hissed. 'Open your mouth.' Irud obediently opened his mouth wide and the warrior stuffed a length of cloth into it. 'Don't speak,' he commanded.

The three Sons of Tuireann hurried Irud through the tall grasses and bushes that lay behind the huge tent, until Brian stopped them. Then he and his brothers joined hands around the terrified king, closed their eyes and concentrated . . . and if anyone had been watching them, they would have seen them vanish as the brothers called down the shield of invisibility!

Surrounded by the shield, with Brian in the lead

111

and Iuchar and Urchar following on behind, they calmly walked through the camp – which was almost deserted anyway, because everyone was on the sea shore watching the metal boat, that was now sailing around in a circle, leaving a foamy white wake. But when it came in towards the shore and it became obvious that there was no one in it, everyone realized they had been tricked, and there was a sudden rush back towards the king's tent.

While everyone ran back towards the tent, the Sons of Tuireann made Irud walk out into the water and climb into the boat. Only one guard, who had had too much to drink, saw the splash in the water and watched the curious movement of the waves heading out – out! – against the tide, towards the metal boat. Then he watched water leap up out of the sea and splash into the boat! The man squeezed his eyes shut and, shaking his head, walked away.

As the Navigator sailed out to sea, the Sons of Tuireann allowed the spell to drop and they became visible once again. Iuchar lit a lantern and hung it on the mast, the soft golden light encircling the metal boat. They could see the king clearly now. He was a young man, certainly not much older than the twins, with pale gold curls and the barest beginnings of a beard on his face. His eyes were the colour of the sea on a summer's day. And he was terrified.

'You ... you're the Sons of Tuireann?' he stuttered.

Brian nodded, without saying anything.

'I know about you. I had a dream warning me about you. You're stealing all the magical treasures in the world . . .'

'Not all the treasures,' Urchar said with a grin.

'Only some of them,' Iuchar said.

'And now you want to steal my dog,' Irud said, his fear turning to anger.

'We would like you to give it to us,' Brian said.

'Never!' Irud snapped.

'You have no guards now,' Brian reminded him, 'and you are many miles from the shore.'

'It's a long swim,' Iuchar said to his twin, not looking at the king.

Urchar nodded. 'A long way, and who knows what creatures lurk in these waters.'

'You wouldn't throw me into the water,' Irud said quickly, appealing to Brian.

'I didn't say I would throw you into the water, did I?' Brian looked at the twins. 'Did I say that?'

'No, you did not.'

'Well, then you did,' Irud turned to the twins, and then looked back to Brian. 'They won't throw me into the water, will they?'

Brian laughed. 'Oh, I've no control over them.' He looked towards the distant lights of the shore. 'But it is a long swim.'

'I can't swim . . .' Irud admitted in a shame-faced whisper.

'What about the dog?' Brian asked.

The king hung his head in defeat. 'He's yours. You can have it.'

As the sun rose the following morning, a small craft rowed by one man set out from the beach with a small basket in it. It rowed to the waiting metal craft where the basket was handed over, and Irud, the king, was helped across from one boat to the other.

Moments later, the Sons of Tuireann sailed away with yet another treasure.

Back in the land of Erin, Lugh, exhausted with the difficult magic of dream-travelling, fell into a deep sleep. And his own dreams were troubled with nightmares about the Sons of Tuireann.

Chapter Eight

The Spell

Lugh awoke with a start.

The young man sat up suddenly; he was covered in leaves, his hair and clothes damp from the night's dew, and images from his nightmare still confused him. For a moment he wondered where he was, and then he remembered he was deep in the heart of the forest that covered much of Banba, beside a pool of icy water.

The young man had been following the brothers' progress first in a magic mirror and then, when he had broken that, in a pool of water that he had enchanted to follow their every movements.

He had done everything possible to stop them after seeing how easily they took the Apples. He had used his magic to make the arrow strike Tuas when they had stolen the Pigskin so they would be blamed for that. He had then warned all the other kings in dreams that the Sons of Tuireann were coming, and had used his magic to prevent the Navigator from sailing back to them when they had taken the Chariot from Dobar. But they had still escaped.

And now he had seen Aesal gift them with the

Seven Piglets, and had watched them trick Irud into giving them the Pup. Two treasures in the one day!

Lugh was almost speechless with rage. When he had given the Sons of Tuireann their seven tasks, he had chosen the seven most difficult things in the world for them to do. He had asked them to find the seven most difficult treasures of all the magical treasures left behind by the Old Gods. He hadn't even thought they would be able to steal the first treasure, the apples, let alone any of the others.

He gritted his teeth and shook his head savagely. But they wouldn't succeed, couldn't succeed – he would make sure they didn't succeed. He needed to make the Sons of Tuireann fail.

Lugh sat beside the pool of enchanted water, his small face pinched into a frown, staring deep into the inky darkness. He was pale and exhausted, his magical attempts to stop the three brothers having drained him of all energy, and there were deep shadows under his eyes. He had the strength left for one more attempt – and this one had to work. They had one treasure left to find and one task to perform. And although the last treasure was the hardest to find and the last task almost impossible to complete – he was going to make doubly sure they didn't find the treasure or shout on Midcain Hill.

Something moved before his eyes and his right hand shot out, snatching a fly from the air. He blew on the tiny insect, turning it to stone and then brought it close to his eyes, looking at it, examining it in detail, wondering at its strange round eyes, running his fingernail along the fine hairs on its back. Flies made great messengers and spies; he had often used them, and because they were so small, they saw and heard everything and no one noticed them.

He brought the stone insect so close to his face that it was almost touching his nose. 'Find my uncles,' he whispered. 'Find Cu and Ceithin.' And then he blew on the fly again, restoring it to life. The fly buzzed around in a circle for a few moments, and then it suddenly shot off through the bushes. Lugh sat back with a smile. The fly would find his uncles and they would join him, and when they had assembled, the three of them would work out a plan for stopping the Sons of Tuireann.

Lugh's uncles arrived a little later, just as the sun was beginning to slip down behind the trees. They were both dark men, and it was whispered that they had some demon blood in them, for they were both very ugly, although Cu, the eldest, was the ugliest. His face looked as if it had been squashed, with a broad flat forehead beneath a mop of wiry grey hair, a nose that was little better than a bump, and a huge mouth filled with teeth that looked as if they had once belonged to a horse. Ceithin, his brother, was not much better. As well as being ugly, he was bald, and had grown an enormous

117

beard that seemed to cover most of his face, and he had combed strands of it up across the top of his head.

Lugh looked up as the two men stamped into the clearing, muttering angrily together. 'You'll have to stop using flies as your messengers,' Cu grumbled. 'This one landed on my food.'

'I'm surprised you didn't eat it,' Ceithin, his brother laughed.

'I did!'

'Uncles,' Lugh stood up to welcome the two brothers. 'Please, let us not fight, we have important work to do.'

'What sort of important work?' Cu demanded.

'We have to stop the Sons of Tuireann.'

'What do you mean "stop them"?' Ceithin asked. 'Surely the tasks you gave them have stopped them?'

'If not killed them,' Cu added, with an evil leer.

Lugh shook his head sadly. 'They have almost completed them.'

'Impossible!' the two brothers said together.

'I'm afraid not. Look.' He gestured into the pool and Cu and Ceithin crowded around to stare into the dark waters. Lugh moved his hand across the surface, and the two men saw the three brothers' adventures unroll before them at high speed. Lugh only slowed the picture down when it neared the end and Irud was climbing out of their boat and they had been given the Pup in return.

119

'We have to stop them!' Cu said.

Ceithin nodded. He didn't speak because he was chewing a mouthful of his huge beard, as he always did when he was thinking hard.

'We could kill them,' he suggested finally. 'Send some foul magic after them . . .'

But Lugh shook his head. 'If they die it has to appear like an accident, and besides, I'm not sure if magic can harm them directly – I think the spell that surrounds the Navigator will protect them.'

'Sink the boat in mid-ocean,' Ceithin growled.

'That would mean losing the treasures they have collected so far,' Lugh said quickly.

'So we have to bring them back to Banba first,' Cu muttered, 'and that's easily arranged.'

'But they're hardly likely to give up their quest right now are they?' Lugh asked.

Cu smiled, showing his huge ugly teeth. 'But they could be made to forget about the rest of their quest, couldn't they? They could wake in the morning thinking their quest was complete, and command the Navigator to return home. When they arrived, we could take the treasures from them – and then accuse them of trying to run away from their quest.' He looked at his brother. 'What do you think?'

Ceithin shook his head in agreement. 'It's an evil and nasty plan. I like it!'

'And when they're here we could kill them,' Lugh added with a smile.

Suddenly both Cu and Ceithin looked doubtful. 'I don't think they'll be that easy to kill,' Cu said. 'See how easily they've gathered the treasures. No, I think it would be better if you forgot about killing them at the moment. Wait until the war with the Fomorians comes. Many will die in that war – and who knows, the Sons of Tuireann might die also.' He smiled cruelly. 'In fact, we could ensure that they would die.'

Lugh nodded. 'So what do we do?'

'We cast the Spell of Forgetfulness,' Cu smiled.

Across the waves, the Navigator rocked on a gentle swell, while the Sons of Tuireann slept easily in the small boat, taking their first real rest for many days. They had one more treasure to find, and one task to perform, and they were confident that they could do both. They would be going home soon.

While they slept, a fog rolled in, a pale white gauze that drifted over the surface of the sea, dulling all sounds, making the world a damp, ghostly place.

The fog drifted around the Navigator, tiny droplets of water forming on the metal craft, little pools gathering in corners. And then, in the midst of all the pale white fog, a patch of yellow appeared, a thick blob about the size of a man's head, shifting, twisting, curling through the thinner natural fog. And whereas the real fog smelt of salt and seaweed, this smelt of rotting eggs and marshy ground. It

121

slithered over the Navigator, leaving dirty greenish-yellow steaks on the damp golden metal and then it settled over the three brothers . . .

The twins talked angrily in their sleep, almost as if they were fighting with one another, and Brian moaned aloud, as if he were in pain, but they didn't wake up. A few moments later, the dirty yellow fog dispersed and the brothers slept peacefully again.

However, as the sun peeped over the horizon, first Brian followed by Iuchar and finally Urchar woke up. They looked at one another, something puzzling them all, but they couldn't decide what.

Brian turned to the Navigator's dragon-prow. 'Take us home, our quest is finished.'

Urchar opened his mouth to say something – and then closed it again. He couldn't remember what he had been about to say. But it didn't really matter, they were going home, their quest was done – wasn't it?

News of the metal boat's approach reached Nuada the King at his palace at Tara. He immediately called for his chariot and rode down to the coast to meet the brothers, followed, of course, by most of the court.

There were hundreds of people lining the sand dunes and gathered on the beach as the Navigator rode in on the waves, with the three Sons of Tuireann standing waving in the prow of the boat. A huge cheer went up as the boat scraped on the stony beach and the three young men jumped out and ran over to their father and sister who were standing in the crowd.

Nuada the King strode over to them, and clapped his huge hands on the twins' shoulders. He nodded to Brian. 'Welcome back.' He sounded pleased to see them. 'You are well?'

Brian nodded, and then raising his voice he said. 'We have completed our quest. We have the treasures.'

Everyone cheered loudly.

And then a thin spiteful voice cut through the cheering. 'All of them?' In the sudden silence that followed, Lugh, accompanied by his two uncles, stepped out of the crowd. The small dark young man looked at the king and said loudly. 'I have looked in the Navigator, and I do not see all the treasures. The Sons of Tuireann are trying to cheat us!'

Brian's sword came out of its sheath so fast that no one even saw him move. He rested the tip against Lugh's chest. 'You lie!' he hissed.

Lugh smiled triumphantly. 'I do not lie, I do not need to lie.' He turned to Nuada. 'Look for yourself,' he said.

The king frowned, sensing something was wrong. He reached out with his metal hand and lifted Brian's sword away from Lugh's chest. 'Let us look,' he said softly. 'I do not doubt you,' he added quickly, seeing the expression on Brian's face, 'but something is amiss here.'

123

Brian nodded slightly and quickly slid his sword back into its leather sheath. He turned to his father and sister and smiled bravely, although he was suddenly very worried. 'Lugh is up to his usual tricks again,' he said softly. 'He tried to stop us on our quest, but we defeated him then, and Nuada will defeat him now.'

Lugh led the nobles down to the water's edge and they gathered in a semi-circle around the metal craft. The young man turned to Brian, a half-smile twisting his lips. 'Perhaps you would like to show us the treasures?' he asked.

Surprisingly, Brian shook his head. 'My brothers will do it.' Brian guessed that something was going to happen and wanted to keep his eyes on Lugh.

Iuchar and Urchar hopped up into the Navigator and began sorting through the treasures.

'You first . . .' Iuchar said.

Urchar shook his head. 'No, you . . .'

'Oh. All right.' Iuchar lifted a large cloth-wrapped bundle and handed it to his brother and then he passed a second similar bundle to the king. Finally he took up a third bundle and opened it – revealing a large golden apple. 'The Three Golden Apples from the Garden of Hesperides in the Orient.'

A huge cheer went up.

Urchar lifted a floppy roll that had been tied with string and undid the knot. A bronze-coloured pigskin unfolded. 'The Shining Pigskin from the Land of the Greeks.'

There was another cheer.

Iuchar lifted a spear and swung it around his head, until its glowing tip burst into flame, and then he plunged it into the water, which immediately exploded into a cloud of white steam that drifted down the beach. 'The Spear from the Land of the Persians.'

The nobles "oohed" and "aaahed" in astonishment.

Urchar leaned out and tossed a small object on to the stones. 'Stand back,' he commanded. The tiny model suddenly moved, and in the blink of an eye it had grown. Another movement and it was larger and larger and larger . . . Finally, a statue of two stone horses behind a stone chariot stood before the Navigator.

Brian leaned forward and touched one of the statues. A whole series of tiny black cracks ran across the two stone horses and the stone chariot, and then the stone covering cracked, small pieces flaking off, chipping away – revealing two real horses beneath. They moved, stamping on the stones, their metal hooves sparking, and the movement shook the last pieces of stone from the chariot, revealing the beautiful workmanship in gold and precious metal. 'The Chariot and magical beasts of Dobar of the Kingdom of Sicily,' Urchar said proudly.

There was another huge cheer and even the guards began stamping their feet and rattling their spears on the stones in approval.

125

Iuchar then passed six small wicker baskets down to his older brother on the beach. He kept the last one and, pulling back the lid, lifted a tiny pink creature into the air. It struggled and squealed. 'The Seven Piglets from the Golden Pillars.'

Everyone was applauding now, even Nuada.

Urchar then reached into the boat and lifted a small, long-haired black dog high into the air. It yapped, wagging its tail happily and twisted its head to lick his hand. 'And finally, the Puppy from the Land of Irud, which will grow into the King of Dogs.'

This time the cheering went on for a long time.

Brian looked at Nuada. 'So you see, we have completed our tasks.'

But Nuada shook his head sadly, just as Lugh burst out, 'You see what they're trying to do? They're cheating. They've left a treasure unfound and a task undone.'

'It's a lie!' the Sons of Tuireann said together.

'I'm afraid it's not a lie,' Nuada said, looking from them to Lugh. 'But something here does not ring true. You think your task is complete?' He looked at them and they nodded. 'You are sure of that?' he pressed. They nodded again.

The king turned to Lugh. 'Has there been magic used here?' The young man turned pale, but quickly shook his head. 'You're sure?' Nuada demanded. Lugh nodded again.

Nuada then looked from the Sons of Tuireann to

Lugh. 'And would you both be prepared to undergo the Test of Truth?' The king raised his right hand and moved his metal fingers, the hinges rasping together. Brian, Iuchar and Urchar nodded immediately, but Lugh didn't move. The king turned to face Lugh. 'You know about the Test of Truth, don't you, Lugh? I will place my right hand – my metal hand – on your shoulder and ask you a question. If you tell the truth, nothing will happen. But lie to me, and my hand will immediately grow red hot, and burn right through your skin to the bone. So, tell me now, do you want to undergo the Test of Truth?'

For a long time Lugh didn't move, and to the assembled nobles that alone told its own story. They began to mutter angrily amongst themselves.

'Answer me, Lugh, do you want to undergo the Test of Truth?' Nuada suddenly shouted, startling everyone.

Lugh shook his head.

'Say it,' Nuada said.

'I don't want to undergo the Test of Truth.'

'Why not?'

'Because I used magic – a spell of forgetfulness – to make the Sons of Tuireann think they had completed their quest,' Lugh said quickly, his voice little more than a whisper.

Nuada turned back to the three young men. 'Because of this evil trick, you may consider that your quest is now complete, there is no need for

127

you to find the last treasure or complete the last task.'

But surprisingly, Brian shook his head. 'No, my lord, we have sworn that we shall recover all the treasures. Tell us what remains to be done and we shall do it.'

'You are proud and honourable people,' Nuada said. 'Your father can be justly proud of you.' The old man Tuireann nodded. 'Very well then, you have one treasure left to find, and that is the Cooking Spit of the Women of Fairhead Island. And you have one task to do, and that is to shout three times on Midcain Hill.'

Brian looked at his brothers, and then without another word, they heaved the heavy Navigator back out into the water and jumped aboard. The dragon's eyes blazed with red light. 'Take us north,' Brian said. The Sons of Tuireann stood in the stern of the boat and waved back at their father and sister, Nuada and the assembled nobles.

'We will be back,' Urchar called, his voice echoing flatly over the waves. 'We will be back!'

And when the ship had sailed over the horizon, Nuada grabbed Lugh with his metal hand and lifted him high into the air. 'And if you attempt to stop or interfere with them, I will have your head!'

Lugh said nothing – but he swore silently to have his revenge. He would find a way!

Chapter Nine

The Last Treasure

The Navigator finally stopped moving in the middle of a cold grey sea and bobbed on the ugly choppy waters.

Brian stood up in the prow of the craft, holding tightly to the dragon's neck, looking all around. 'Where are we . . . where is Fairhead Island?'

Urchar, who was sitting in the bottom of the boat, looking sick and miserable, shook his head. 'There is no such place as Fairhead Island. There is a headland called Fair Head on Banba's northern coasts, but there is no island of that name.'

'There must be,' Brian said.

Iuchar stood up and joined his brother. Unlike his twin, he didn't suffer from seasickness, and the motion of the ugly, heaving sea didn't bother him at all. He pointed off to the right, 'What is that land there?' he asked.

'That is the land of the Scots,' Urchar said in a whisper. He closed his eyes tightly, as the world began to shift and turn around. He was going to be sick again he knew.

Iuchar pointed to the left to a grey smudge on the horizon. 'And what is over there?'

'That is Erin's coasts,' Urchar groaned. He wished his brothers would just leave him be.

'Then it must be here somewhere,' Brian said slowly. He raised his voice slightly. 'Navigator, take us to Fairhead Island.'

The dragon's eyes blazed bright red, but the metal craft merely turned around in a complete circle.

'Well, the Navigator thinks this is it,' Urchar said.

Brian crouched down beside his brother and put his hands on his shoulders. 'Urchar, you must tell us what you know of Fairhead Island.'

Urchar groaned.

Brian closed his eyes and concentrated, and Urchar suddenly felt his sickness ebb away and new strength flow into him. He looked up to find Brian staring at him, a smile crinkling the corners of his soft grey eyes. 'Feel better now?'

Urchar nodded. 'Much. I don't like this rough sea,' he admitted.

Brian nodded and patted his shoulder. 'It's nothing to be ashamed of; we all have something which distresses us. I'm not really too keen on thunder and lightning myself. Now, you must think, you must concentrate, and tell us what you know of Fairhead Island.'

Urchar nodded. 'Fairhead Island. Yes. I've heard

of it in some of the ancient tales. There is a story of an island between the coasts of Banba and Alba, an island that was destroyed because of the evil ways of its inhabitants.'

'How was it destroyed?'

Urchar frowned, shaking his head slowly. 'I don't know . . . something about fire and water . . .'

'Think, brother, think . . . it's terribly important,' Iuchar said.

'I'm thinking . . . I'm thinking,' Urchar snapped. 'Just leave me be for a moment.'

Brian touched Iuchar on the arm, and they stepped back, giving their brother space and time to think. Long moments dragged by, while Urchar rocked gently to and fro, humming softly to himself, his eyes squeezed shut. Suddenly, he sat forward, his eyes snapping open.

'It sank beneath the waves!' he said excitedly. 'The ancient sagas say that "the Isle of Fairhead in a day and a night vanished beneath the sea, consumed by Manannan, the Lord of the Sea".'

'But why did this happen?' Iuchar wondered.

'Because its people practised such foul magics.'

'And what treasure are we looking for now?' Brian asked.

'The Cooking Spit of the Women of Fairhead Island,' Urchar replied. 'Anything cooked on this magical cooking spit will never end. A chicken might feed an army of ten thousand, for no matter

131

how much is taken from the chicken on the spit, plenty will remain.'

'So . . .' Brian looked over the side of the craft into the murky waters. 'It seems we must look down for this island.' He looked at his brother. 'Does it exist?'

Urchar tapped the metal craft with his foot. 'Well, the Navigator seems to think so.'

Brian nodded. 'So it's down I must go.'

'Don't you mean "we"?' Urchar asked.

Brian shook his head. 'No, this time, only I will go down, you two will remain here to give me strength with your magics.' He saw their puzzled looks and continued, 'We draw our magic from the Land of Erin, and to perform any great magic we must be in sight of Erin's shores. Well, if I'm below the surface of the water, I won't be able to see the coast, now, will I? So you two will have to draw upon your magics and direct it down to me.'

'But why you?' Iuchar asked. 'One of us could go.'

Brian smiled. 'Urchar gets seasick – and you cannot swim under water, remember.'

Iuchar turned red and nodded his head. He could swim on the surface, but he hated putting his head down, hearing the roaring, bubbling, pounding in his ears, feeling the stinging salt in his eyes.

Brian turned to his younger brother. 'What will we need for this spell?'

'Well, for a spell of this kind, you'll need some seaweed,' Urchar said decisively. He lifted a long spear from the bottom of the boat and passed it to his twin. 'Catch as many long strips as you can.' He turned to Brian. 'Will you wear a rope around your waist?'

Brian started to shake his head, but suddenly nodded. 'Yes, I think I will. If I get into trouble I can tug sharply on it and you can haul me up.'

Iuchar, who was dragging a batch of stringy, smelly seaweed over the side of the metal craft, looked up. 'But we don't have a rope long enough . . .'

Urchar looked crestfallen. 'He's right . . .'

Their older brother laughed and ran his hands through the twin's flaming red hair. 'Don't you worry about that, that's easily fixed.'

'How?' Urchar demanded.

Brian leaned over and plucked a hair from Urchar's head, making him squeak in surprise. 'I'll make a rope of human hair.'

Iuchar laughed. 'But that's hardly strong enough.'

'It will be when I work a spell on it,' Brian smiled. Now, let's hurry, we have work to do.'

So, while Iuchar dragged the seaweed into the Navigator, Urchar untangled it and then cut the weeds into long thin strips with his knife. Brian meanwhile, having plucked a handful of hairs from his brothers' and his own head, was slowly and carefully tying them together to make a long, almost invisible, thin red thread.

133

'I'm finished,' Urchar said suddenly, looking around, surprised to find that the thin strips of seaweed had grown into quite a bundle.

'So am I,' Brian said. 'I'll work my magic first I think,' he added, lifting the almost invisible thread into the air. He stood up in the boat with his left hand outstretched before him, the thread resting across the palm of his hand. He raised his right arm to the sky and then turned his hand so that his palm was facing upwards. Closing his eyes he called upon the Dagda and Danu, the Great God and Goddess of the Celts, to aid him.

For what seemed like a long time nothing happened, but then, very distantly, thunder rumbled. The thunder came again almost immediately afterwards and it sounded closer now, and then it grumbled again and again, coming nearer all the time.

Suddenly there was a terrific boom, and the three brothers jumped, for the thunder was right over their heads. They looked up to find that a thick grey-black cloud had gathered above the Navigator's mast, and as they watched, lights moved within the cloud.

Then, in an explosion of light and sound, a thunderbolt streaked from the clouds – directly on to Brian's hand!

The long rope of hairs glowed a bright, brilliant red and the smell of burning, scorching hair made the brothers cough and their eyes water. When they

134

could see again, the thunder cloud had gone as suddenly as it had come, and in Brian's hand lay a hard red-black thread that shimmered with a distinctly metallic sheen. And when Brian dropped it on the deck of the Navigator, it tinkled like metal wire.

Brian stripped off his weapons, clothing and sandals and stood quite still while the twins wound the long strips of seaweed tightly around his body, covering him from neck to foot, leaving only his head free.

Urchar then took a long strand of seaweed that was covered in air bladders, which were like hard little bubbles of weed. He broke one of the bladders and, with the tip of his knife, made a tiny hole in it. Touching it with his index finger and calling upon the Old Gods for help, he brought the bubble to his lips and blew gently into it – and the bladder inflated! The soft greenish-brown nodule expanded to the size of a fist, then grew larger, then to the size of a human head.

Iuchar, seeing his brother become red-faced, reached out and touched the huge bubble with his finger, hardening it.

Urchar sat back gasping. 'I can see spots before my eyes,' he complained, handing the hard bubble to his older brother.

Brian lifted it and brought it down over his head – and it fitted perfectly. Iuchar then wound another length of seaweed around his neck where

135

the hard bubble joined the rest of the strands of weed.

As the twins watched, the bubble, which was still a dirty greenish-brown colour, began to change, the muddy colours becoming pale and then finally vanishing altogether, leaving Brian staring out through a clear hard helmet.

Brian reached out with both seaweed-wrapped hands and took hold of his brothers' hands. Standing in a circle, they called upon Manannan, the Lord of the Sea, to help them. But nothing seemed to be happening – until Urchar noticed that the seaweed covering his brother's body had hardened to a crisp, armour-like shell. Brian released his brothers' hands. 'It's done,' he said simply.

Without a word, Iuchar tied the metal thread around his older brother's waist, and Urchar checked the knot. Brian put a hand on both their shoulders and squeezed hard and then he smoothly dropped over the side of the Navigator into the cold grey waters of the northern seas.

The twins looked at one another, but they didn't say a word. They didn't need to, they knew they were thinking the same thing: would they see their brother again?

The waters closed over Brian's head and for a moment he almost panicked, then he felt the cold seaweed that was wrapped around his body grow warm, and he knew the magic was working. He opened his mouth – he had been holding his breath – and breathed deeply, and tasted cold, slightly salty air. The magical helmet was working, sifting the air from the water around him.

He sank deeper and deeper. It was pitch dark now and he was completely blind. Things brushed past him, he wasn't sure what – and he wasn't really sure he wanted to know, but he smiled, imagining the shock for the creatures that inhabited this watery world at seeing this strange invader drifting through their 'sky'.

Time had no meaning here, so when he finally saw the light below him, he had no idea whether he had been falling for a few moments, or for a day or even a week.

The light below him was soft and green, and seemed to be drifting through the inky sea like bands of coloured fog. He fell through one of these bands – and the whole world lit up in colour. Scores of fish – some large and dull-coloured, others tiny and beautiful – darted past his face, while weeds and strands of grasses moved all around him. Thousands of creatures moved through these weeds; tiny star shapes, clouds of darting specks, even tiny horse shapes . . .

And then he fell out of the band of colour and was blind again.

But the sea bed was below him now; he could see it clearly because this green cloud seemed to cling to the ocean floor. Brian looked – and then looked again. What he had first taken to be rocks and tumbled stones were actually buildings, still standing but all covered in weeds and barnacles which helped to disguise their shape.

He had found Fairhead Island.

His feet touched the ocean floor, little puffs of sand and grit drifting up, sending crabs scuttling away. He stood for a moment, allowing his eyes to adjust to the light again, wondering what he was going to do now.

He tried to make sense out of the shapes of the buildings all around him. It was difficult because the outlines had been hidden by the weeds and silt that had built up around them. He wasn't sure, but that shape there – a roughly square shape of grit and stone, covered in weed and shells – might have been a large building when this place had rested above the water. And he knew that in the older villages it was usual for the food to be prepared in one main hall. Well, it was a place to start . . .

Although the hall looked close by, his every step was a weight, and he was exhausted by the time he reached it. He went around the building three times, but could find no door, nor anything that even looked like a door, so he finally drifted in through a window, carefully pulling in the red wire behind him, lest it get entangled.

He turned – and stopped in horrified amazement.

There were people in the hall, dozens of people. There were men, women and children, all of them

138

wearing skins and leathers, and all clearly from another time. There were even a dozen huge hounds lying before what must have been the hearth, although it was now nothing more than ashes.

And they were all frozen solid.

A broad table of rough wood stretched down the centre of the room, and there were people sitting on crude stools, obviously waiting for their meal. Or at least they had been waiting for their meal when the disaster had struck all those hundreds of years ago. They were all frozen stone-still in the positions they had been in then. It was like a hall full of statues, but very life-like statues indeed.

The young man moved cautiously down the hall, looking at the people. Brian wondered who had done this – who had the power to do this, and more importantly, why had it been done? What had the people of Fairhead Island done to deserve this?

He reached the end of the room – and discovered his answer. The hall had been built on two levels and on the lower level there was the cooking spit he had come looking for – a huge crude thing of beaten metal. There were three old women seated around it, one with her hand still on the spit, the others frozen in the act of passing her more meat. Beyond these three old women and the cooking spit there was a huge pile of bones – human bones. The folk of Fairhead Island were cannibals. That was why they had been destroyed.

Brian stood for a long time looking at the three women of Fairhead Island and the cooking spit. It consisted of two 'Y-shaped' sticks and a long bar that rested between them. The meat was stuck on the long metal bar that rested between the two sticks and then slowly turned over a fire. Knowing what it had cooked, he was very reluctant to touch it, but he knew he had no choice. He had to bring it back.

Brian reached out and plucked the long pointed bar first, and then pulled up the two sticks. He was turning away when the old women moved, turning their heads to look at him. They smiled, opening their mouths, showing long sharpened teeth. Brian turned to run – and found himself facing a hall full of awakened islanders, all smiling, all showing their long yellow teeth. They shuffled forward, raising their hands for him.

Brian took a deep breath, gripped the pieces of the cooking spit more tightly – and pulled on the metal thread around his waist.

And far, far above, the twins felt the pull, and knew something was wrong. They had prepared for this. They had wrapped the rope around the metal body of the Navigator. 'Spin!' They both shouted. And then Navigator began to spin at high speed, wrapping the thread around its body.

A huge bearded man reached for Brian, his nails long, pointed and dirty – and Brian was abruptly wrenched forward!

He flashed past the man's outstretched hands and was moving so fast that people just bounced off him. Two warriors, wearing the skins of animals that had long since died out in Erin, stood before the window he had come through, blocking the way, long staffs in their hands. Brian turned his body, so he hit them sideways on, sending them crashing backwards into the wall while he went shooting out through the middle. There was a grating, rumbling sound as bricks gave way and then the whole side of the building collapsed in a cloud of sand, and dirt.

As Brian was pulled upwards, the building collapsed in on itself, trapping the awakened cannibals within – and immediately the soft green light died also, leaving the ocean floor to its natural darkness.

Iuchar and Urchar hauled Brian out of the water, tossing the Cooking Spit into the bottom of the boat without even looking at it. They were more concerned for their brother.

Urchar cut away the seaweed and pulled off Brian's helmet. 'How do you feel?' he asked anxiously.

'Dizzy,' Brian said, and immediately fell asleep.

Chapter Ten

The Final Task

'So we only have one task left to perform,' Iuchar
said as they sailed away from the cold seas above
Fairhead Island.

Urchar glanced over at his twin and nodded. He
turned to look at Brian, who was sitting huddled
in his cloak in the stern of the boat, his hands
wrapped around a goblet of steaming hot mead.
Urchar turned back to his brother. 'You know,' he
said, 'I think this will be the most difficult of all.'

'We gathered all the treasures,' Iuchar protested.

'But the last one nearly killed Brian,' Urchar
said, lowering his voice. 'And surely Lugh knew
that? And why do we need a magical spit that will
make food last forever? We already have Seven
Piglets that can feed an army of thousands. No,' he
shook his head. 'I thing Lugh deliberately sent us
after the spit knowing that the enchanted
islanders would awaken when someone
attempted to take it away. What would have
happened to Brian if he had not been tied to the
Navigator? What would have happened if they had
caught him . . ?'

'They would have killed, cooked and eaten me,' Brian said, startling them both. 'And then, once awakened and fed, they might possibly have floated their island back to the surface again. I might have been responsible for creating an island . . .' he smiled bravely, but the twins could see how tired and drawn he looked.

'You should rest,' Urchar said. 'We don't have far to go.'

Brian nodded and settled back down into the boat, with his back to the mast. 'Where are we going, and what are we going after?' he asked.

'We're going to the land of the demons themselves, the land of the Fomor. It's a cold chill place, covered in snow and ice and with huge moving mountains of ice floating in the seas that surround it.' Urchar turned and looked ahead into the sea, which was now a dark angry grey, flecked with whitecaps. 'We have one task to perform,' he continued slowly, 'and that is to shout three times on Midcain Hill.' He turned around to look at his brothers who were still and silent, watching him. 'You remember our father said that it was guarded by four of the demon-folk, Midcain and his sons, Corc, Conn and Aedh.'

Brian nodded. 'Yes, I remember he called it the Hill of Silence. The demon-folk ensure that no one speaks loudly on it.'·

Iuchar sighed. 'And we have to shout.' He looked from Urchar to Brian. 'Could we not just shout quietly from the bottom of the hill?'

Brian looked shocked. 'We are the Sons of Tuireann. We shall shout from the very top of the hill.'

Iuchar nodded. 'I thought we might.'

'There is one other thing,' Urchar said softly. 'We only have two days left. You remember Lugh said the Fomorians would attack Erin in twenty days?' They nodded. 'Well, that was eighteen days ago. If we are to succeed, we must complete this task tomorrow, the nineteenth day, because it will take us another day to return to Banba.' He stopped and suddenly pointed to a white and silver mountain rising up out of the sea. 'That's it, we've arrived.'

They rested in the Navigator that night, shivering beneath their cloaks in the chill northern air, sharpening their weapons, for they knew there would be a fight on the following day.

None of them thought they would sleep, but as the night wore on and the sharp brilliant points of starlight faded slightly, one by one they fell into a deep restful sleep. And they all dreamed of the soft green fields of Erin.

The morning was bright and sharp, and the air was so cold it burned in their lungs. Brian called for the Navigator to move in towards the shore. At first he thought the metal craft was not going to be able to move because ice had built up around the craft overnight, trapping it. But the Navigator shuddered, the dragon's eyes blazed a deep, fiery red, the ice split and cracked all around it and then, slowly but surely, it moved in towards the shore, ice crackling and splintering everywhere, the noise echoing and re-echoing off the towering sheets of ice.

'Well, at least they'll know we're coming,' Brian smiled. He was standing in the prow of the boat, studying the hill ahead. 'Now, it looks like there is only one path to the mountain top, so here's what we'll do. You two will guard the path – it's fairly narrow and you should be able to keep even these demon-folk away from you. I'll climb up to the top and shout, and as soon as you hear me shout, be prepared to fight your way back to the boat because the Fomor will come running then.'

'What will you shout?' Iuchar asked.

'Oh, I'll think of something,' Brian said with a grin.

The beach was rocky, and the rocks were covered in a thin layer of ice, making walking difficult, but once they got up off the beach the land smoothed out, and the first signs of a track became visible. As they moved away from the rattling of the stones on the beach, the hissing of the sea and the constant creaking of the ice, the first thing they noticed was the silence.

There was no sound on Midcain Hill.

Even though the slopes were covered with a light blanket of snow, it was obvious that all the vegetation had been cleared away. There were no

146

bushes, no stunted trees, and the snow itself was clear and unmarked, with neither bird nor animal tracks.

Midcain Hill was a dead place.

'It's eerie,' Iuchar said, his voice falling to a whisper. He shivered, even though he was wearing his heavy woollen cloak, and he kept turning around to look behind them.

'Let's get this over with as quickly as possible,' Urchar said, his teeth beginning to chatter. Like his twin, he suddenly felt frightened.

Brian nodded. He shaded his eyes and squinted against the glare from the snow, looking up the hill. 'There is a tall standing stone there,' he pointed. 'I'll shout from there. You two stay here and keep a close look out. I'm sure we're being spied upon.'

The twins nodded, and turned around to guard the path. They were both carrying spears, and wearing swords and knives.

Brian continued on up the path, his sword in his hand now. The snow wasn't as deep this high up, but there was ice beneath the dusty white covering and he had to test every step before moving. When he finally reached the standing stone on the brow of the hill, he was panting and slightly out of breath. He leaned against the pillar of stone and looked back down the hill to where his brothers were standing guard.

From this height – although the hill was not

147

very high – he could see out across the Land of the Fomorians, ice-white and sparkling, the lakes blue-cold and frozen. This was a dangerous, deadly land, he knew, and he could certainly believe that the people who inhabited it were demons . . . but he had to admit, with the sun glinting on the snow and ice, making tiny rainbow patterns everywhere, it was a very beautiful land too.

Brian straightened up and looked at the pillar of stone. It was tall, far taller than he was, three-sided, and down the edges of one side were a series of lines and nicks cut into the stone. Brian touched the marks with his fingertips; it was Ogham, the secret writing of the Druids, the Holy Men. He wished Urchar were there, he would be able to read it with no difficulty. However, he would have to make do as best he could. Touching each line and mark with his fingertips, he slowly spelled out the words . . .

"Let no man disturb this sacred peace . . ."

Brian smiled, well, he was about to disturb the sacred peace. He opened his mouth to shout . . .

There was a flicker at the corner of his eye and he dropped to the ground – just as a huge battle-axe chunked into the stone, sending chips flying.

Brian rolled to his feet – as two creatures appeared before him, one with an axe, the other wielding two swords, one in each hand. They were the Fomor. They were huge hairy creatures,

148

almost completely covered in fur, except for their hands, which were like human hands, and their faces, which were human too, except for the fact that they had only a single eye in the centre of their foreheads. At first Brian thought they had no mouths, but then he realized that they had strips of cloth wrapped across their mouths – probably to stop them from speaking accidentally, he guessed.

The first demon attacked again, swinging his axe in low and bringing it up sharply. If it touched him, Brian knew, it would cut him in half. He threw himself backwards, rolling to his feet again – just in time to meet an attack from the second, the younger, of his two attackers.

One sword sliced at Brian's head while another went low. Brian deflected the higher sword with his own, and then jumped on the blade of the second sword, trapping it beneath his boot. And when the man attempted to pull it free, Brian kicked him with his other foot, the flat of his boot catching him low in the stomach, pushing him backwards. The demon's arms swung as he attempted to keep his balance, and then he was gone, tumbling helplessly down the hill in a cloud of snow and ice.

Brian turned to face the axeman.

The twins heard the clash of metal and turned in time to see Brian kick the swordsman down the hill, and then turn to the other demon. They

149

looked quickly at one another and were about to race up the hill when two more of the demons appeared directly in front of them, literally rising up out of the snow. They must have been hiding there all morning, remaining still and unmoving, just waiting their chance while the brothers walked all around them.

Iuchar thought they were furred demons, but Urchar recognized them as ordinary men wearing clothing of thick furs. The only difference, as far as he could see, was the fact that they only had one eye, and he wondered how they could see. Did they see as clearly as ordinary human beings, or did they see more clearly at night, or was it perhaps to enable them to see in this blinding snow . . ?

But he hadn't time to consider it any further, because the Fomor attacked. They were both carrying tridents, long poles with a three pronged fork on the end. It was a fisherman's tool, used for stabbing fish or larger sea creatures.

One jabbed at Iuchar, and the blades of his trident actually passed through his cloak, becoming entangled there. Iuchar swung his own spear, catching the creature on the side of the head with the butt end, the force of the blow snapping the wooden shaft in half. The creature stopped, looked at him for a moment, and then his single eye slowly closed. Iuchar turned to help his brother, who was in trouble, when the man Brian had pushed off the top of the hill crashed into him, sending him sprawling.

Meanwhile, Urchar was up against a dangerous opponent. The demon was fast and very strong, and Urchar – who was more of a scholar than a soldier – had already been cut twice on the hands and arms, thin shallow cuts which didn't bleed much, but which stung like fire.

The man kept jabbing, jabbing, jabbing, and Urchar kept blocking with his spear, but he knew it was only a matter of time before the demon managed to stab him. He couldn't out fight him, so he would have to out think him . . .

The creature had only one eye, so . . .

Urchar began to shift around, slowly at first, moving away from the creature, and then when the demon was forced to move in to stab with his trident, he began to turn . . . turn . . . turn, until eventually, he had traded places with the creature. He fought with him then, knocking away the trident as it jabbed and stabbed. And all the time he was counting, slowly and carefully . . .

And then the sun's ray lanced over the top of the mountain straight into the creature's single eye! The demon was blinded – and Urchar killed him with a single blow of his spear. He turned to help his brother, but Iuchar was climbing out from under the still body of the demon. He was bleeding from a cut on his forehead, but otherwise seemed unhurt.

152

The twins turned and ran up the hill to help Brian.

Brian was facing Midcain, the Keeper of the Hill. He was a wily and dangerous fighter, very fast and wielding his huge battle-axe as if it weighed no more than a stick. Twice he had cut so close to Brian that he had nicked his skin, slicing through his clothes, and only the young man's speed had saved him.

Brian was wondering how his brothers were faring; he had no worries about Iuchar, he was a fighter, but Urchar was a different matter. He had to kill this demon now and hurry down to help his brothers. He attacked, his sword darting, stabbing, slicing, cutting ... but Midcain was fast – very fast – and his thick furs protected him. Brian had touched him at least four times with his sword, but each time his flat sword blade had bounced off the demon's furs.

Midcain glanced down the hill – just in time to see the twins racing up. He turned back and attacked Brian with added rage, hacking with his axe in both hands, cutting, chopping, spinning his axe in a blur of steel around the man, forcing him back ... back ... until he was up against the cold stone of the pillar.

Brian fought all the harder then, but his arms were tiring, they felt like lead and he knew the demon was going to kill him. He saw the axe rise up and then come swinging in fast and hard. Brian

153

tried to raise his sword, but knew he would never make it in time. So he did the only thing he could – he fell to the ground!

The axe struck the stone with a clang that sent echoes rattling over the hill. A huge chunk of granite was torn away, ripping through the line of Ogham writing, breaking the magical spell – and then the stone blazed with an intense cold blue light. The metal head of the axe burst into a thousand fragments of molten metal. The shock sent shivers running up Midcain's arms, numbing them, up into his chest, numbing it, stopping his heart in shock, up into his head. The demon saw blue light, harsh, sharp, painful blue light, blue . . . blue . . . black . . . The demon closed his single eye – and died still standing on his feet.

The twins ran up, their weapons ready, pointing at the huge man, but he was still and unmoving. Brian climbed to his feet and looked closely at the demon. 'He's dead,' he said in wonder.

'When he damaged the stone the old magic in it probably killed him,' Urchar said slowly. He was feeling dizzy and his tongue felt thick and large in his mouth. Large black and coloured dots were drifting across his eyes.

'Let us shout,' Brian said, and then he suddenly shivered. His wounds were stinging. He turned to stand beside the shattered stone and raised his head.

'I am Brian,' he called, his voice echoing and re-echoing over the snowy landscape.

154

'Iuchar,' his brother called.

'And Urchar . . .'

And then together they shouted, 'We are the Sons of Tuireann!'

One by one they slumped down beside the broken stone, suddenly feeling terribly tired and weak. 'What's wrong?' Iuchar gasped.

'My wounds,' Brian said, touching the scratches on his arm and chest. They were burning with a cold fire.

'Poisoned!' Urchar said abruptly. 'Their weapons were poisoned. We're dead.'

'We must get back to the Navigator,' Brian gasped. 'It can take us back to Erin, and then the Three Golden Apples can save us.'

Iuchar began to shake, 'But will Lugh give them to us?'

'He has to,' Brian said confidently. 'Our quest is done.'

Chapter Eleven

Eithne's Tale

I am Eithne, the Daughter of Tuireann.

My father Tuireann and I were waiting on the beach for the metal boat when it finally appeared over the horizon on the morning of the twentieth day.

We knew they were coming, but nothing else. In our magical mirror we had watched them go up the hill to fight the giants – and then it had suddenly cracked. We could only pray that they were well.

The boat crunched up onto the sand and then lurched slightly to one side and the red fire in the dragon's eyes died. For a moment my father and I didn't move – we were almost afraid to look inside, and then a hand appeared on the edge and Brian's head came up. I almost fainted when I saw him; I know I cried aloud. His face was pale and thin and there were deep black hollows under his eyes.

'Poisoned,' he whispered through his cracked lips.

Our father nodded. He first helped Brian lift the

twins out and placed them side by side on the sand. They were breathing loudly and looked pale and their red hair made them seem even paler. Brian sank down on to the sand beside them, folded his arms across his chest and closed his eyes.

I watched as my father lifted his long staff and ran it slowly up and down their bodies, his lips working, calling on all the healing spells he knew. But I knew, even as he was doing it, that it was useless. This was demon poison.

Finally, my father looked up. 'Only one thing can save them now,' he said slowly, his voice cracking. 'The Golden Apples from the Garden of Hesperides.'

'Will Lugh give them?' I asked.

'He has to,' my father said decisively.

'But you will never get to Tara in time,' I protested.

The old man smiled. 'I will,' he said.

He drew his cloak up around his shoulders and hunched his head down, and then as I watched, he seemed to shrink in on himself, becoming smaller and smaller. The cloak changed texture, the rough cloth sprouting feathers, the feathers growing, lengthening, and then falling back – revealing a sharp-beaked black raven. The bird cawed once and took to the sky, heading north, towards Tara and Lugh.

I sat with my brothers then, watching them

through the long afternoon, waiting. The sky was darkening for night when the bird appeared flying low in the deepening sky, and I knew immediately that it was carrying nothing.

The bird dropped from the sky – and turned back into a man before its feet touched the ground. 'He wouldn't give them,' my father said, almost in disbelief. There were tears in his eyes and the disappointment was bitter in his voice. 'After all they did . . . and he wouldn't give it to them. I nearly drew my sword and ran him through . . .'

Brian's eyes flickered open and we both knelt by his side.

'He wouldn't give us the Apples . . .' Tuireann said, his voice harsh and hoarse.

Brian nodded. 'I know,' he whispered. 'It is his revenge.' He closed his eyes for a few moments, and when he opened them, there seemed to be a new strength in them. 'Put us back in the Navigator . . .'

My father and I carried the twins back into the metal boat and then we helped Brian in. He looked at my father and although his eyes were full of pain, he smiled bravely and said, 'When the name of Lugh has been forgotten, everyone will remember the name of Tuireann.' and then he raised his head and said, 'Navigator, take us to a place where we may be cured . . .' The dragon's eyes burned and the boat shifted on the sand and turned back towards the sea. Brian looked at me and said, 'We will be back . . .'

And so they sailed away.

I have walked this beach for many years now, waiting for them to return. And they will return some day. I know they will. I know they were cured.

And as for the Treasures – why, it turned out they could only be used by those who had claimed them. No one could bring out their magic, not even the finest magicians in the land – only my brothers could have brought forth their magic.

I am alone now. My father is dead – he never recovered from the shock of losing his three sons at the one time. But I have lived long enough to see Brian's prophecy come true.

The name of Lugh is almost forgotten now, but the Legend of the Sons of Tuireann lives on . . .